WHO ART IN HEAVEN?

Ilyas Iftikhar

First Edition
© Ilyas Iftikhar 2017
@ilyasiftikhar

Paradox Books
London

ISBN: 1527209393
ISBN 13: 9781527209398

British Library Cataloguing-in-Publication Data
A catalogue record of this book is available from the British Library

Printed and bound by CreateSpace USA

Dedicated to all those slain in the name of faith

CHAPTER ONE

I t was early morning on 10th October, 1999, when I was shot dead. I vividly remember the thumping of about a dozen feet as they ran down our corridor. My mind was half-asleep and half-awake. I had put my alarm to snooze a few times, but the thumping was what actually alarmed me. Whenever there was such commotion in the hostel, especially in the early hours of the morning, chaos was destined to follow. I sprang out of my bed to check that my door was bolted so that trouble could be avoided. Within those few seconds that fell between the sound of thumping feet and me jumping out of my bed, my mind was busy anticipating what could have happened. It wasn't a very hard puzzle to solve as only a few options entailed such raids. It could be that someone had gotten on the wrong side of the right wing JTI. These three letters were a puzzle for many. All they knew was that the combination of these three letters stood for terror. It was wall-chalked all over the campus. *Free Aslam Bhai of JTI or be ready for the consequences. Allow JTI to hold their conference or see the campus ablaze. Fire Professor Khan or JTI knows what to do. Get burqas to be part of female uniform or JTI will fix it.* It was all about *ifs* and *thens*. All about threats. All about terror. All about fear. All about violence. In truth, the wall-chalked slogans had nothing to do with the actual affairs of the University. Only a few such slogans would have *Jamiat-e-Talaba-e-Islam* instead of the abbreviation. *The Union of Students of Islam*, as it literally meant, was the ruling student union and the only pressure group, at Punjab University, Lahore.

As my mind ran through the tangled anticipations, I felt the breeze of a late autumn wind. Autumn in Lahore does not symbolise gloominess as it does in the western world. For Lahorites, it means the dying away of a scorching summer heat that had grilled them for a good six months. It means the ever-perspiring pores of their skins can now rest after a long phase of being hard at work. They can finally go out in the *Bagh-i-Jinnah* on The Mall or Racecourse Park on Jail Road for an afternoon stroll with their families. They can finally enjoy sitting in a restaurant and enjoy their food and drink without the blazing heat of summer spoiling the mood. Although dating openly was full of risks in a so-called Islamic society, lovebirds could still find ways to be together in the picturesque gardens of Lahore. Autumn means that pigeons, held for *kabutarbazi* on the full-of-life rooftops of traditional Lahore, can take longer flights after a long season of sizzling heat. It means that the infamous load-shedding won't be cursed at when it left fans and air-conditioners impotent of bringing down the temperature. In our campus, autumn meant much more. It meant that girls would now be seen more frequently walking along the famous canal that stretched like a spine through the strong, handsome body of the campus. Hanging branches of the willow trees bowing to touch the pacified water of the canal always seemed mystical. Tips of the branches would peacefully stay dipped in the waters, only moved by the ripples formed by passing boats that floated past occasionally.

It was the breeze of this beautiful autumn that brushed my body and sent a wave of life through my mind and soul as I hastily got out of bed. I was in a state where one's mind feels overwhelmingly preoccupied when they suddenly wake up, like multiple windows opening on the desktop of a computer. I remember that my mind quickly thought about my unplanned day ahead. The image of my loving mother also appeared in one of the windows on my mind. Among those thoughts was the thought of the hostel fees that were due and had to be paid immediately.

All this, but in the flash of a few seconds. My hand ran to the bolt on the door. It was locked. But the thumping stopped right at my door. My name was being shouted, paired with all sorts of profanities. *Oi.* Salik. *Kuttay. Ghaddar. Kanjar. Haramzade.* This was followed by many more swear words, some very graphical and obscene. *What on earth...! I can't take all this.* I flung the door open. I had to find out, so even though I was only dressed in a sleeveless vest and *shalwar,* I decided to get out to see what was going on. I remember about six or seven fully-bearded men standing before me, dressed in *Shalwar-kamiz,* traditional white *topis* on their heads, sticks in hands. A typical bunch of *JamiaJamiatt* fanatics stood right in my face. One of the Maulvis thrust forward, gun in hand, *'Allah-u-Akbar! Labbaik Ya Rasulullah!'*

That was about the time when I was shot point-blank. I only remember seeing the goon raising the gun to my forehead. I can recall the sizzle of the bullet that penetrated my skull and how I hit the ground.

Other than that, I remember that it was a beautiful morning, in the beautiful campus, in the beautiful city of Lahore.

I could hear the bunch of religious hooligans walk away. They didn't even feel the need to run. I could still hear their murmuring, as they passed comments on their accomplishment. The sound of their feet thumping on the corridor and then on the stairs faded away. Only then could my hostel-fellows from my neighbouring rooms dare to come closer to see what had happened. A whole crowd of students, startled and shocked by what had happened, stood at my door looking down at me. I was lying in a pool of blood that slowly grew larger. My eyes were wide open, and blood gushed out from just above my right eyebrow. My vest stained by the spray of blood that shot out as soon as the bullet hit my forehead. My *shalwar*, all creased and wrinkled as I had only just woken up. As I had fallen back, my wagging arm had hit my study table bringing my books and the mug that I used as my stationary holder down to the floor. It was a very loyal mug that had been with me since college. Now, it lay in shards all over the floor. My pens, pencils, highlighters were all over the place, on the floor and on my bed; an eraser and few other items lay on my chest.

Then came the sound of sirens. There was an ambulance station within the campus, and they had been called to the scene. They came and waited for the police because the paramedics had said that they could do nothing before the police gave the go-ahead; yes, very ironical but this is the Pakistani way of dealing with emergencies—from personal to national or even international.

It took the police an hour and a half before they handed my body back to the paramedics. There seemed to be no rush because anyone could tell that I was dead. There were no vital signs, so there was no point rushing any procedures. I remember how the paramedic had let my cold hand fall back to the ground when he had determined that I was clinically dead. My cold hand hit the puddle of blood making a small splash, enough to get a drop of my blood on his shoe. He rubbed his shoe against my *shalwar*, as he walked past me, to get rid of the small drop of blood. I was no more so he thought that I could be treated like a doormat. He wasn't wrong. There was no life in me. I was completely cold.

The police tried to cordon off the first floor of the hostel where my room was. But in Pakistan, a mere blue and white tape is never sufficient to cordon off a crime scene. It has to be a human chain which meant about three mobile units of the Muslim Town Police Station being sent down to the campus. SHO Gulab Khan was heading the initial investigation. The many policemen who had come to attend the crime scene and to cordon it off stood here and there holding batons in their armpits. I lay cold and still in my room as forensics took photographs of my body and my room. The forensics handed over the body to the paramedics, one of whom came forward and shut my eyes that had been gazing at the ceiling for the last three hours. I was moved to a stretcher before a white sheet was placed on my body. I was carried down the stairs very carelessly, the only care being that the body didn't fall off the stretcher. Whether my body reclined or my arm dangled off from the stretcher was no one's concern. As I was taken out of the hostel building, I could smell the cheapest brand of cigarettes. A policeman, unfit as a rhinoceros, smoked the cheap brand of cigarettes, K2 with smoke puffing out of his nostrils. This had made the grey hair of his moustache turn pale. As he snapped off the ash occasionally, some of it landed on his mouldy toes that peeked out of his sandals. The strong smell of this cheap brand reminded me of my own pack of Dunhill that was in the left pocket of my blue jeans that were hanging on my door-peg managing somehow not to fall off the huge bulk of clothes that always hung behind the door. The very handsome packet of golden and maroon combination. *How many were left in the pack? Probably half a packet full.* I smiled at the thought that it was by this time in the morning that I would usually light my first cigarette. After my breakfast and a lovely cup of tea, I would inhale the first puff of the first cigarette of a brand new day. What a feeling it was. But now, there were no breaths, so no more cigarettes. How sorry I felt for myself, only smokers can imagine.

CHAPTER TWO

I was born in Faisalabad, a city in the Pakistani Punjab about ninety miles west of Lahore. The earliest memories I have of my childhood are shrouded in a haze of religion. Everything I remember from my early childhood is somehow connected to religion and faith, maybe because Islam overwhelmingly characterised the atmosphere of our household.

We lived in a joint family comprising of my grandfather who I called Dadaji, grandmother who was Dado for all of us, two uncles with their wives, their children and us—Mother, who I called Ammi, Father who was Abbaji and I. Our house was a traditional Punjabi mansion, or *haweli* as it is called. Red-brick walls, red-brick outdoor staircases, front courtyard with red-brick flooring with a series of arches on the wall that led to the veranda. The grandeur of the *haweli* did not necessarily depict a wealthy living; it only spoke of a glorious past and a fortunate inheritance for too many to share.

All rooms were beyond the veranda. Beautifully carved wooden chairs lay around in the veranda for onlookers of the rich Punjabi culture that thrived in the vast courtyard. The courtyard had *charpai* beds lying around, occupied by the various residents of the *haweli* who would be engaged in various activities all through the day.

A usual day in the *haweli* started with my dad and uncles taking turns to wash-up at the basin that was fitted in one corner of the courtyard, followed by combing their hairs and beards. Then the three wives of the three brothers would serve them breakfast on the *charpais* in the courtyard (and in the veranda in winter). Abbaji and his brothers would then go to their rooms to change into the neatly pressed *shalwar-kamiz* suits that their wives had ironed while they had breakfast. Then the three brothers would sit with their mother in the courtyard for a little while as she would give them her blessings before they left for the seed shop that their father, my Dadaji, had established in Aminpur Bazar when he had settled in Faisalabad after the bloody partition of India. The shop was not a very big one, but the business was fairly successful. My father occupied the shop while my uncles would travel to deliver orders made by the farmers in the agricultural lands that lay around Faisalabad. They would sometimes stay out for a night or two When they travelled to distant locations.

It was the veranda and the courtyard where all of us children would get ready for school. My female cousins had been taken out of school as soon as they touched adolescence as was customary for girls in many areas of the Muslim subcontinent. They were the ones who got us, the younger cousins, ready for school while our mothers submissively, yet happily, served our fathers their breakfast and packed their lunch. We were made to recite customary Arabic prayers as we started to eat, finished our meals or even burped as we ate. We were made to memorise prayers for leaving the house, entering school, stepping into the mosque, leaving the mosque and even for returning home every time we did during the day. We had to recite them out loud for our elders, who were custodians of our faith. Those who forgot to do so were penalised. The penalties were soft-core, like saying the missed prayer ten or twenty times or even more if you were frequently forgetful of this religious duty.

We would wake up very early as the day started with the pre-daybreak *namaz*. This would be followed

by Dado, Abbaji, Ammi and uncles and aunts all reciting the Quran in tunes that they thought were
melodious. So, the chanting of Arabic verses from
dawn to dusk was a background sound for every act
of the daily drama, although we hardly ever bothered to ponder over the meanings.

The second act of the daily drama in the courtyard and veranda started with us, the boys and men,
having left for school and work. This act, which
lasted until midmorning, was when all the girls and
women at home had breakfast; dunking every bit of
their *paratha* or bread in hot tea sided with even hot-
ter gossip.

Midmorning would see vegetables chopped and
spices ground for the afternoon meal. Dado loved
to do this job, but her daughters-in-law would join
her. Then as the meal would be cooked by the wom-
en, the girls would clean the courtyard, brushing the
red brick floor with a broom and sprinkling water to
settle the dust down for the rest of the day.

Then came midday along with the rise in temperature which, during most parts of the year, would
gradually get unbearable as midday turned into
noon and noon into afternoon. The scorching heat
of Punjabi climate would make the red bricks on the
walls and on the floor absorb the heat and radiate
it up to late afternoon and even early evening. The
heat would send everyone indoors, which usually

meant that the airy and shady veranda where ceiling fans would propel, occasionally stopping with the load-shedding of power, would provide a temporary shelter. These fans gave more noise than air, as they roared at full speed.

Around this time, we would arrive back from school. A noon-nap, or siesta as you would call it in Spain, was almost a must-have for us youngsters. So, we would quickly change out of our uniforms, have our afternoon meals and tuck into bed or lie on the bare floor of our rooms for a nap. It was during those hot hours that the theatre of the courtyard would be called off. But by late afternoon, it was time for more acts to be played in the courtyard. Us youngsters were made to take a bath and rush to the mosque where Maulvi Saheb would teach us to read the Quran. These lessons were tough. A single mistake could get you smacked, because not reading the Quran correctly was a grave sin in the eyes of Allah, and even more so in the eyes of Maulvi Sahib. We would get severely punished if we made mistakes, and this, unfortunately, happened too often.

Those lessons are a very important chapter of my childhood memories, bringing with them an unpleasant whiff of fear because it was those very lessons that first gave birth to questions in my mind which I never had the courage to ask. *Why am I reading a language that I can't even understand? Why do I read parts of it in my five daily prayers almost fifty times a day when I don't even know what I'm saying? Why would Allah be happy with me chanting some verses in a strange language that I don't even understand?* I would never feel like reciting the Quran for the mere reason that I had no understanding of any of it. Since everyone else around me seemed content, I sometimes thought that maybe there was something wrong with me. Since they didn't ask, it seemed as if they didn't think about it. This was when, for the first time, I developed a feeling that perhaps it was not normal to be the way I was. Only once did Daud, my cousin, refuse to go to the mosque for these lessons and that too for the very honest reason that he didn't quite understand what was being read and memorised; and that he didn't like Maulvi Sahib. What he got in return was not concern or sympathy from his elders or even empathy, but a good thrashing. This left me with no other option but to suppress such questions because voicing them was blasphemous.

So, I grew up not knowing the meaning of the Arabic that was chanted and sung in each of the five daily prayers that punctuate the day of a Muslim. I chose not to ask, as I didn't want to commit sin. Daud was told that he had committed blasphemy and would be sent straight to hell for asking such a question if he did not repent. "The way to repent", he was told, "is to repeat this prayer thirty thousand times". This left me with further questions. I thought repentance is meant to come from within, not without; but for this sin, or crime, the repentance too was imposed and enforced. *Is Daud really repentant or is he just pretending to be? Would this act even help in avoiding the hell that otherwise awaited him?* His crime had been to proclaim that he couldn't make sense of a language that was foreign to him and the punishment for such a crime was to repeatedly chant more from the same language. *Has Daud got his answer? Would this penalty enable him to understand the language?* I brushed these questions off and tried to carry on with what I was expected to do because I really did fear the terrifying god that I was introduced to; the god that my family called Allah! The god that was angry and furious about anything and everything; the god that didn't care for our sentiments but only for his own; the god whose height of delight was to see me washing my face with cold water before every *namaz*; the god whose only concern was money, money, money; the god that got pleased when we, frail human beings, praised him, the 'almighty'; the god that could make us rot in hell if we forgot to wear a *topi* for *namaz*; the god that could give me a terrible illness if I, even as a very young child, took my gaze off the prayer mat during *namaz*. Yes! I was very frightened of this god. The fear etched on my mind by my parents, kept me from asking any more questions. My submission made me the natural favourite of Ámmi, Abbaji, aunts, uncles and grandparents alike. I was a "good boy" who said all his prayers, read the Quran daily, chanted all the Arabic verses with every movement that I made during my waking hours. I enjoyed this reputation of mine and didn't want to ruin it by a question that brought back no answers.

The occupants of the *haweli* would see us youngsters playing different games and sport, as Dado told us off if our ball hit her or when we laughed or screamed too loud. But our sport and her telling-off both went on, and we all enjoyed this lively atmosphere. The freedom in the courtyard during those evenings is probably the best memory of those days. The fun would end with sunset. We would then be told to run off to the mosque for evening *namaz*. We would grab our *topi*s, shout *salam* at the top of our voice repeatedly as we ran to the mosque chasing each other and playing tag. After saying the *namaz*, we would sit and listen to Maulvi Sahib as he gave a brief sermon afterwards.

I must say that I learnt a lot of good things from those post-*namaz* sermons of Maulvi Sahib. It was a great help in character-building. He talked about respecting elders, helping those in need even if it was trivial or even if it meant going out of our way to do so; spending on those who were poor and most needed the money that we would otherwise spend on toys or things that account to luxury. He would explain how important it was to be kind to those younger than us. I strongly believed that Maulvi Sahib was a practising, staunch Muslim who practised everything he preached, except kindness to younger ones. I couldn't make sense of how his sermon and his beating up of the children could be reconciled. But then I thought that a pious man like him, as we all knew him, would at least enjoy this much exception in the law of god. So what, if five-year-old Ajmal had Maulvi sahib's fingers printed on his face when he got slapped for not reading the Quran right? Maulvi Sahib, I would think, was at a position that he knew best about our faith and, well... Ajmal was Ajmal. But I never gave it too much thought and importance, with the fear that negative thoughts about even Maulvi Sahib could be taken to be the same blasphemy that Daud, my cousin, had committed and got severely reprimanded for. So, I stayed away from thinking too much.

By the time we would get out of the mosque, it would already be dark, and we would run home to avoid falling victim to crimes that our elders had told us stories about. Fear brought us straight back home; the same fear that is used to control millions of human beings in the world.

By the time we would get home, the characters of the courtyard theatre would have retired. I can still feel the melancholy that would strike as soon as we walked through the front door at night into an empty courtyard. The courtyard that would buzz with love and happiness all day long would now be a dark patch of emptiness as the night grew in. All that was left to be done was to have a few bites of supper, chit-chat with the cousins and then to bed. Mother would lie down with me and make me revise all the Arabic prayers that I had committed to memory. I would say them aloud. I still remember the glow on her face when I got them all right. She would hug me, kiss me and say all the good things that a mother could about her child. She wasn't bothered if I had understood them or not. All she knew was that Allah must be happy with her son who had got all the Arabic right.

CHAPTER THREE

Childhood is probably the best part of one's life, and like all good things, it simply slips out of your hands like grains of sand. Growing up in the *haweli* was a lot of fun. Many phases came and went: marriages, divorces, births and deaths. But life went on as normal.

I remember how Dadaji's death had brought thick clouds of sorrow on our *haweli*. Every one of us, the dwellers or characters of the *haweli*, were deeply saddened. Abbaji, being the eldest son, seemed to be the one most moved by Dadaji's death. The shop in Aminpur Bazar had stayed shut for a good couple of weeks as if it would never open again. Dado seemed to have almost died with her beloved lifelong companion. It seemed as if she would never come back to normal; and if Dado didn't come back to normal life, that would mean the whole *haweli* would seize to exist with all its energy and buzz. The television never got switched on for months after Dadaji's death. My cousins and I never even dared ask permission.

Emotion and its expression are two integral parts of Punjabi culture. I would actually call them one because one doesn't exist without the other. Family feuds could erupt if a relative had not sufficiently expressed their grief at a funeral or even by failure to show enough joy at a wedding. So, with all the other learned behaviours that a child picks up from his surroundings, we as children had learned to express sorrow and to show that we were equally saddened, even if we actually weren't.

So, there was no question of turning the television on or even asking about it. Authority of all kind, traditionally and culturally speaking, lies with the father in a Punjabi, or rather Pakistani or actually, Indian society. Whatever he says, goes. I knew that one fine day when Abbaji would finally feel like watching TV, he would start off by saying, *Let's see what the news says* and that would bring the television back to life. And that is exactly how we got our television back.

I feel that the grief of Dadaji's death had faded out of Abbaji's heart in a few days' time but what took him even longer to come back to normal life was its standard expression. I was too young to worry or even think about all this, but I now feel that their business must have suffered, with the mourning being unnecessarily prolonged over months. My father and uncles all stayed home during that time of self-styled mourning, attending to visitors that poured in to pay their condolences. I would see the same people coming in, again and again, lifting their hands to pray for Dadaji. *Are they really that sad at the death of a person who happened to be just a neighbour?* I would wonder. Various rituals were performed during all this period of mourning, all in the name of faith. Every afternoon, Abbaji, my uncles, my male cousins and I would visit the grave of Dadaji, lay flowers that were bought on our way to the graveyard, raise hands to offer prayers, and, most surprisingly, leave a bowl of *halwa* by his headstone. Little did I know that the denomination of *Sunni* Islam that I belonged to, only by birth though, required that the deceased be offered the food they liked in their life for the first forty days after their death. In my ignorance, I asked,

"Abbaji, does Dadaji know we bring this *halwa* for him?"

"Of course he does!" Abbaji replied, with a hint of astonishment.

"Does he eat it?"

This was naturally my next question. A very innocent question. My father stayed quiet as if he hadn't heard. Repeating a question to an elder was taken to be rude. A 'good boy' as I was, my father didn't expect that I would repeat my question. But I was, after all, too young, and even more curious.

"Abbaji? Does he eat it?" I repeated as I walked behind him.

With a pause, he replied, "Of course he does!"

Does he really think so? I asked myself. *Do all these wise elders, all think so? Or, is it me again being silly, thinking that the foxes, stray dogs and rats fed on the food laid beside his headstone?*

I began getting feelings of guilt. *I must be so bad! How blasphemous it was for me to think that the food left for Dadaji was eaten up by beasts in the wilderness of the graveyard.* Why the bowl we had left the previous day was always toppled over with *halwa* scattered all around as if Dadaji had gobbled it in a rush, would have been my next question. But I just brushed it away.

So, it took months for the family to recover from the bereavement. Life got back to normal. Dado, who everyone thought was too emotionally disturbed and felt lonely after Dadaji's death, survived him for ten years. I was in primary school when Dadaji died, and I was preparing for my final year at college exams when Dado passed away. She was the focal point of our *haweli*. If the *haweli* was a body, then she was the soul. Everything seemed to revolve around her. She was a larger–than-life type of personality. She played old style games like *barataini* draughts with us, sang and danced at weddings of her grandchildren, told jokes, or rather created a joke out of every situation, the latter being her speciality. I always thought that the day died would be the day the *haweli* would dis-integrate. It could continue to be an abode but not a hub where a whole culture of love, peace and joy thrived. I had always hated to imagine living in the *haweli* without Dado, and I felt that I would not be able to live in such a *haweli*.

I was lucky that she died only a few months before, I too had to leave the *haweli*. She died when I was preparing for my final college exams. These exams would lead me to apply for admission to universities, and that would mean leaving Faisalabad and move to some other city of Pakistan. However, her death proved a bit untimely because the rituals surround-ing the bereavement took too much of the time that I had wanted to spend in preparing for exams. What made it even more challenging to attend the rituals was that by that time, I had lost faith in God. The god that was behind all those rituals. Every single ritual was to please the god who sought pleasure in everything from birth to death. I couldn't tell this to anyone, not even to my own self, that I no longer believed in god. So, I decided to stay in the closet.

I felt extremely sorry for my parents who had spent all those years trying to instil in my heart the belief and love of a god. I felt that I had wronged them badly. So badly that I could never even tell them of the ordeal I had gone through in this journey from 'belief' to 'disbelief'. What would have been even more painful for them was to find out that my loss of faith was primarily because of them. They had introduced me to a concept that my mind had rejected just as a new born baby rejects and ejects any distasteful object from its mouth. If our DNA is designed to accept certain types of foods and reject others, the same is the case with concepts and ideas which get accepted and rejected by our minds. The concept they had introduced in the name of god had been unacceptable for me all along. I had tried my best to accept it, to live it and to love it, but had failed.

It was in school that I first realised that I did not want to believe in god. I kept telling myself that there was something wrong with me but eventually reached the conclusion that the matter was otherwise. There was something wrong with the concept of god that my parents, teachers, uncles, aunties, cousins and our Maulvi Sahib had wanted me to believe in. I decided to keep my doubts locked away in the closet by performing all rituals that were expected of me; not because I wasn't bold enough but because it would have meant calling for trouble, which I didn't want to stir up at that time.

I had decided that I wanted to excel in life and this decision had brought my studies at the top of all priorities. I blamed illiteracy for the defected personalities of Abbaji and my uncles; defected because they always decided to stick to ritual and not common sense. I felt that that could never result in a normal life; a life we are expected to live in a society, by the society, or even by their god. Apart from this major reason, I must admit that there was a certain feeling which I would not call fear but something closer to anxiety that was associated with the very idea of giving up belief in god; the type of anxiety that accompanies the giving up of a lifelong habit or an obsession. Belief in god, for me, was more of an obsession than a belief, hence, questioning it came with a feeling of anxiety from which I did recover, but it took its time.

So, while all rituals around Dado's death were performed, I would physically be a part of it though my mind was more focused on my studies than the sorrow that I had always dreaded. She had prayed to her god for my success until her last breath. I really appreciated her passion but wasn't really convinced to believe that her prayers were actually getting registered somewhere, let alone being accepted. For me, her prayers were like the steam that shoots out of a pressure cooker; it makes a sound, it's hot, it gets felt but soon evaporates in the air and is no more. I did feel the warmth when she would hug me and pray to her god for me, but I would feel no different as soon she had stopped chanting prayers and blowing her prayer-laden breath on me. That breath that had a whiff of the pieces of food sitting under her dentures, but I didn't quite mind it.

She strongly believed, like all staunch believers, that saying prayers and blowing them on me would actually protect me and go with me a long way. For me, it was sacred only because those breaths came with her warmth and love; nothing more than that. I missed her a lot, but my studies did not let me get carried away with the tragedy because I knew that there was no second chance for me.

'If you don't do too well in exams, why bother wasting money on university fees? Just join the business' Abbaji told me on many occasions, and I knew that he meant it.

My male cousins who had not done well in studies were now helping out at the shop. Why they had not done well was nowhere in the equation for anyone. Their failure had provided Abbaji and uncles with the cheapest labour, and my cousins with an easy living. They went with their dads and came back home with them. They got food from the combined meal that was always cooked in the *haweli* and had no utility bills to pay from their own pocket. No needs were left as such, but they still got some stipend, probably to keep them from hunting jobs elsewhere. The fear of being part of the family business for the rest of my life was something I dreaded a lot, and that dread was a major factor that pushed me to put more effort into my studies.

If I did ever imagine myself taking up this family business, I would plan it like an enterprise not a sole-trader shop in the Aminpur Bazaar of Faisalabad. I would watch ads of fertilisers and insecticides on television that targeted farmers and agriculturalists and would daydream of having a similar business if I was to end up in the career that I least desired.

Despite my interest in economics, I had purposely avoided taking it as a subject for my degree because I knew that Abbaji would have then insisted that I got into Agricultural Economics at the Agricultural University of Faisalabad thence leading to a career in agriculture and ultimately to the family trade. Getting admission in a university in Faisalabad would also save him the money he would otherwise have to spend on hostel accommodation, food and travel but I wanted to move out of Faisalabad. I could not live all my life in a place which was more than a village, less than a city yet nothing like a town. And Lahore had always been like a heartthrob for me. Several visits to Lahore with my father when he would go to wholesale markets had left a very deep impression of Lahore on my mind. As a young boy, I couldn't grasp the reason for the attraction, but as I became more sensible, I got to understand that it was its strong cultural decorum that had left a very pleasant image of Lahore.

I opted for political science and philosophy as my major subjects in college. I knew that Political Science could be an option that my father would agree upon and let me pursue a career with a hope that it might bring some good to the family repute. But philosophy would have been a straight rejection. He wouldn't let me invest my time and his money in a subject that was of 'no value' as he would put it for anything that had no commercial value. Anything to be valuable in his eyes had to be of immense religious or commercial worth and value. So, anything that could bring great commercial benefits in this world or ensure a ticket to the paradise in the next was what mattered to him, and anything between the two was not even important. I sold him the idea that a degree in political science could open ways for taking a public service examination to join foreign diplomatic service of Pakistan. The prestige associated with public service jobs, especially the foreign service, the financial security and, above all, the very handsome salaries were the factors that helped me sell the idea.

I had never been too friendly with my father as he had always played the role of a mini-god and I gave him the respect that I should have given to god. I would remember that I had missed my prayers as soon as he walked through the threshold of the *haweli*'s front door. I would do many 'virtuous acts', rituals rather, only because I knew Abbaji was going to enquire and not because god wanted me to do them. When he found out that I had said my prayers on time and Maulvi Sahib told him that I was being a good boy at Quran lessons, my father would be over the moon. I could see the pleasure in his eyes as he felt proud of me. It was all about pleasure! God wanted to be pleased, my father wanted to be pleased, but the difference was that I could see Abbaji's pleasure, but with god, I never really knew.

I had been told as a child that even if I was going to the mosque to offer prayers, but I put my left foot first in the mosque and not the right one, Allah would not accept my prayers and would be very unhappy. So, you never really knew whether this god, my parent's god, could ever be pleased. But father could be pleased, and I could see him happy. Then father was the provider of our daily bread, he was omnipotent when it came to family and *haweli* affairs, he was the almighty when it came to finances, so he was more of a god for me than the unseen one. I felt overawed to talk much to my father. Our conversations would usually be initiated by him, or I would speak to him only when it was inevitable. My burning desire to get into the Punjab University, Lahore left me no escape, and I had to talk to him about it.

"Okay. If you think you can become some big-shot ambassador or minister, then maybe it's worthwhile. Otherwise, I don't see the point in going for political science. I didn't raise you to be a politician."

That was his reply. I could tell that he wasn't too happy, but the permission I required had been graciously granted by this demi-god of mine. I didn't want anything more.

The two weeks between Dado's death and my exams flew past in a blink of an eye, and so did the exams. I had a feeling that I had done well and my results proved me right. I had secured first division in both Political Science and Philosophy, but I knew that I was only applying for a place in Masters for Political Science.

CHAPTER FOUR

Packing my bags for Lahore, I felt for the very first time how deeply affiliated one can be with a place where their childhood is spent. The *haweli*, the peoples' colony where we lived, and the town of Faisalabad, all seemed to be holding my hand, asking me not to go. They were all deeply embedded in my heart. Pleasant memories kept tossing and dancing on the canvas of my mind; some vivid, some in silhouette. Whatever the image from my memory bank, the soundtrack in the background remained the buzzing sounds of talking, singing, shouting, laughing and sobbing of the *haweli*. There was no Dado to sit me by her side and blow her prayers on me. She was with her god, supposedly living the eternally happy life that she had always expected to welcome her after death. Ammi had been very quiet for the last few days. She only spoke when spoken to. The grandeur of Abbaji's personality kept her from even expressing her emotion at her dear son departing. The only rare occasions when she had spoken out were drenched in emotion, trying hard to hold back her tears.

"Can you not apply here in Faisalabad? The business is good enough; why not just join; you've studied enough, haven't you?"

I knew where she was coming from. I knew exactly what she meant. I just pretended that I didn't because what lay between the lines was mere emotion and not much thought. It was not that I didn't care for her emotions. In fact, I knew that further education would make her beloved son a better person, and this would be far greater happiness for her than me simply staying and joining the family trade. I would hold her hand and tell her that I really should study further or all the years gone into my education would go in vain. I would console her by promising that I would visit home frequently. I would try to cheer her up by telling her to pray for me. *Me, requesting prayers!* I actually felt sorry for her that she believed in the wonderland of prayer and its acceptor. She wanted me to progress, but she wanted it to happen only through prayer and no practical effort. She lived in no different a tragedy that every believer lives in; *Allah Malik Hai! God will take care of everything.*

Abbaji had not acted much differently than usual in the days that approached my departure. He was the same godly figure; indifferent from his own creation, happy with the feeling that he was strong and all others were weaker. So, Abbaji didn't show any emotion. However, I felt a strange attraction towards him, something I had never felt all my life. I had started to notice every act of Abbaji more closely. I could feel he too was emotional, but its expression would have brought him down from the lofty status that a father enjoys; the godly status of being supernatural and aloof from anything human. I would find him gazing at me whenever I accidentally caught his eye, which he would hide by abruptly starting a conversation as if he was about to say something anyway.

"Listen, try not to squander all your money. Live within your means. There is so much in Lahore to divert attention. Don't get carried away!"

But I could feel the warmth in his gaze that I would catch. We both wouldn't express our emotion; we had never done so, and we probably could never. I had, for the first ever time in my life, felt a great surge of earnest gratitude for my father. He had looked after me well. He had been my provider, and although I always saw him as a miser, he had never deprived us of any basic need.

Apart from Ammi and Abbaji, the only other thing holding me back, as if to stop me, was not a person but the *haweli*; the *haweli* that was more of an institution than mere bricks and mortar. The buzz had been on like always, but as the days of my departure drew nearer, everything seemed to go in slow motion. The wind, the sunshine, the peculiar smells of food cooking in the kitchen, the occasional whiff of stench that came airborne from the sewage holes, the walls, the open-air staircase that led to the roof-top, the clothes waving on drying lines, slippers lying stranded around the courtyard and the constant, or chronic, clip-clop of water drops dripping from the tap in the courtyard had always been there but it was as if I was feeling their detail for the first ever time. Everything seemed to have a character. It was as if I had discovered the pulse of the *haweli* throb with all its life and spirit. Unlike Ammi, it did not say anything in words. It was wiser than Abbaji as it didn't try to hide an obvious expression. The *haweli* had been more sacred, more godly. It never broke its silence. I felt the warmth of the love for this beautiful *haweli*, which I thought would soon start to crumble and finally collapse because Abbaji and my uncles were too sensitive about having it renovated. The renovation would have meant bringing down the rooms where Dadaji, and then perhaps Dadaji's Dadaji had breathed their last. It would mean losing the veranda where Dado and her predecessor Dados had spent their sleepy, drowsy, lazy afternoons. I only wished that the *haweli* stayed intact forever, but I knew this was, but, only a wishful dream. Buildings and their architecture can express our emotions but cannot hold them and stand on them forever. Mughal Emperors like Shahjehan, Humayun and Akbar never understood this fact when building tombs and monuments in love of their wives and mistresses. So, I didn't expect laymen like Abbaji and my uncles to be any cleverer.

On my part, it was hard for me to bid farewell to the *haweli*; only the *haweli* because for me the *haweli* had my Ammi and Abbaji as an essential part. The *haweli* was representative of an era of my life; an era that was now rapidly drifting into the past. Missing it would mean missing a lot of elements of my life. I had always thought that I was not plagued with emotion like most Pakistanis but those moments, when I packed my bags to finally depart, gave me second thoughts about myself. I got to know that day that emotion and culture cannot be surgically removed. Culture is not as benign as we think it to be; it is deeply rooted in our psyche, and it will strike whenever it gets even the smallest of openings.

I did not buy new bags. Ammi would always have solutions to such issues. She pulled out some very old-fashioned, dusty bags from underneath her bed, emptied the fancy clothes she had stuffed into them from the time of her wedding, sunbathed them and the problem was solved.

"These should be perfect!"

So she thought! Besides, who was I to disagree? I was the one who never really cared about looks. I had a very strong aesthetic sense but my aesthetic sense looked deeper than the skin, or so I thought. I didn't have much to take with me. A couple of *Shalwar-kamiz* suits, and vests. Boxer shorts were not in fashion in my time, town or family. It was later in Lahore that I was to wear western trousers and realise that what seemed to be an extra was actually a necessity. A towel, some toiletries, a couple of bed sheets and a pillow case on which Ammi had very fondly embroidered my name in Urdu. As I gave final touches to my packing, Ammi asked if I had spare space in my bag. She wouldn't look at me while she asked this but I could see tears waiting to burst out of her eyes and roll down her cheeks. Ignoring her emotional state I responded in the affirmative. She walked very briskly into her room and came back with a cardigan.

"I knitted this for you. I heard it gets really cold in Lahore. Wear this, even if it's only slightly cold."

Ammi's geography, history, astrology and any other form of knowledge, whatever small amounts of it she had, was based on hearsay. She was completely illiterate. Her only qualification was whatever she had been told by her father before marriage and then my father afterwards. I only smiled at her innocence.

"Ammi, it's only Lahore. I am not going to London. Okay fine! I'll wear it. I'll tell you what, I'll put it on now. It's getting quite chilly!"

This made her laugh as I said this in a blazing summer's day. But with this laughter, she lost control of all emotions and the tears she had been holding back for days finally rolled down her cheeks. She broke down and wept. I hugged her. I hugged Ammi after years and years. The last time I hugged her was when I was young enough to beg Ammi to tuck me into bed. The warmth of her motherly love crept into my soul. She just hid her face in my chest and wept. She didn't say a word; neither did I. Aunties and my female cousins didn't know whether to intrude in this mother-child affair or to just leave us alone. But they couldn't afford to behave indifferently because, like I said earlier, not sharing an emotion could lead to family feuds. So, they stood at a distance, saying consoling words only make to make it felt that they weren't unmoved. Ammi wept on my chest for quite a few minutes, but those minutes seemed to span over years. I don't know how much longer she would have wept had it not been for the roaring of Abbaji's motorbike that always announced his arrival. She moved away, wiped her tears and ran to her room to compose herself. Her god had arrived, and this god didn't like people to seem unhappy. He wanted to see them only happy regardless of whatever the true feeling.

"I'll drop you to the station. I'm going to say my *namaz*, and then we leave."

It was the first time in many years that this statement hadn't followed the question whether I had said mine or not. I thought I should because I knew it made him happy. Whether god would be happy or not, I couldn't care less. I didn't even want to know. This last *namaz* that I offered before my departure was probably the only *namaz* that ever gave me some degree of satisfaction. Or maybe it wasn't the *namaz*; I am sure it was the hidden pleasure that I had seen on Abbaji's face as I walked out of the room folding away the prayer mat and putting it away with my *topi* on Dado's wooden bed in the veranda. But this pleasure didn't last long. The god in him didn't let him be pleased for too long. He took his eyes off my face and looked down at the *topi* that I had put away. I knew what that meant. I picked it up and put it in the front pocket of my bag.

I didn't want to meet Mother again, but I had to. I went to her and bowed my head. She put her warm hand on my head, her other hand holding my hands. It was for the first time that I noticed how her skin was ageing. She never looked old to me before that event. She kissed my forehead and tied a charm on my arm. She said it had the strongest verse of the Quran wrapped in the small leather satchel tied to a black string.

"*Ja Beta!* This *Ayatul Kursi* will protect you."

All I knew about this *Ayatul Kursi* was that the word *Kursi* means chair in Urdu. I didn't know anymore nor did I want to. *How could some words, written in a language I didn't understand, protect me? Protect me from what? How? What if I wanted to indulge in something myself? Would they hold me back?*

But that was only for a split second. I had declared a ceasefire in my philosophical war on religion; I had no desire to go into it again. I said *Salam* to my aunties, uncles and cousins. Daud seemed sad to see me go. Aunty Amna gave me a box of Halwa she had cooked for me to take along. Uncle Ashraf gave me a hundred rupees, and Uncle Ali thought his prayers were enough.

I walked out of the front door of the *haweli*.

"*Bismillah...*"

Abbaji always said this spell phrase as he kick-started his motorbike.

I sat on the back seat of his motorbike, clutching my bag and off we went towards the railway station.

I looked back at the *Haweli*. I was leaving behind the *Haweli*, which meant leaving behind Ammi, uncles, aunties, cousins, many memories and, above all, the god that had lived with me in the *haweli*.

It was hard to say what dominated my mind; the sorrow of leaving behind the culture embedded in me or the joy of moving to the beautiful, vibrant, buzzing city of Lahore. I was very anxiously looking forward to being in University. I felt that the foundations of a bright future and the romance of the university awaited me and I was pacing closer to both with every passing moment.

CHAPTER FIVE

I t was a very pleasant morning in August when I woke up in my room in the Noor Uddin Zangi hostel. I could see the canal enveloped in rows of trees stretching along its entire length. This canal ran through the campus dividing the campus into educational blocks on one side and the residential halls on the other. My roommates were students of the same batch but not my class fellows; Saleem from Gujrat going for a Master's degree in Geography, Akhtar from Chiniot in Philosophy and I, Salik Hussain Qadri in Political Science. We, three complete strangers, were to become good friends in the days to come, but that morning, we were strangers and didn't have much to say and share. Introductions usually fill such voids, and it did so very aptly. We went to the mess for breakfast and had a good chat introducing ourselves to each other. Both of them said that they had made it to a highly esteemed university only by the grace of Allah. I listened with great interest, with tongue-in-cheek though, as I picked up the feeling that I wouldn't miss the *haweli* much. The god I thought I had left behind in the People's Colony of Faisalabad had decided to accompany me to Lahore. But I had always respected other people's faith in god as it was something very dear to them. They didn't believe in god, they actually believed in a concept that their parents had named so. But so what? I too believed in so many things that I had never seen or experienced.

Walking out of the mess, I thought of the fortunate ones studying in Cambridge, Oxford and Harvard. Those were even more esteemed universities than Punjab University, and a majority of those who made it to these universities were non-believers. Whose grace must have taken them there? But such thoughts were only undercurrents of everything I did in my everyday life. It wasn't like I always intended to delve into such thoughts or entertained them all the time. They came and went like thousands of other thoughts that cross our minds, thousands of times a day.

The predominant thought was the pleasure I got from this beautiful morning. The hustle and bustle of university life in that bright morning, the walk along the canal to my department, the solemnly flowing water of the canal, the flimsily dancing branches of willow trees kissing the water with their leaves, the fresh air with the scent of flowing water, the steaks of light making their way through the leaves that played with the breeze and, above all, my ambition to succeed in life; all of this left a deep impression on my heart and soul as I walked towards the lecture theatre in the Department of Political Science. The grandeur of the university had embraced me fully. I could feel the sense of belonging to this university already. As I walked through the vast corridor leading to the lecture theatre, My confidence made me feel taller than I actually was. University buildings are designed to instil in you a feeling of pride. They are made to seem great so that they remind you of the great people that once walked the corridors, sat in the lecture theatres, indulged in great discussions and had tea at the cafeterias as they smoked cigars and wrestled with great ideas. I was overawed by the feeling of my presence in the atmosphere where I felt in the air the scent of knowledge and wisdom.

Is there anything bad I remember about this morning? Not that I recall. Or actually, yes! One thing that broke the spell was the wall chalking here and there. Political slogans were written in bold and ugly graffiti on the walls by JTI. I didn't know what this JTI exactly stood for, but I wasn't really too curious because news bulletins usually mentioned them in the news of riots and strikes in colleges and universities. So, I had an idea that it was some kind of a student union but I also I knew I would have nothing to do with it as I never had been a political activist in my college days. One more thing to leave that beautiful morning blemished were the names etched on the pillars that carried the roof of that beautiful corridor. Names, mainly of boys and some of the girls but the latter seemed to be written by boys as an expression of fantasy. This left a bad taste but the aura of that beautiful August morning was much stronger to suppress any stupid thing that stood in its way.

In the lecture theatre, every face was new. We were all strangers up to the time that a lecturer walked in.

"I'm Dr Saleh, and I'll be teaching you *Modern Political Thought.* This is paper three of your curriculum. But we won't just start today. We need to know each other first. Let's start with the girls."

He said this with a twinkle in his eye. Many other eyes twinkled to appreciate the wise decision of Dr Saleh.

The introduction started. In such formal group introductions, I would hardly ever remember names.

The body language, the accents, the intonation and other non-verbal elements stayed with me as a better introduction to a person. There were twelve girls in our class, but only two caught my attention. Not because both were good looking but because they were as confident as a falcon in flight. I had grown up seeing women who seemed oppressed, depressed, careless about their looks and timid. I admired the confidence the two girls spoke with.

"Shamaila Ali. From Kinnaird College. Second class in BA. Best tennis player at college for two years."

This was jaw dropping for me. A girl who could not only play tennis but also be the best player in the game. *Wow!* I was stunned.

"Farah Abid. Government Islamia College for Women, Gujrat. First class in BA. President of the debating society at college. First position in debates at inter-district level competitions."

Uh-huh? Interesting! I looked in astonishment.

Anyone could guess she was a debater. She was full of conviction. *Great stuff!* I never knew women could speak this boldly in the presence of men. Ammi and aunties would open the door to the milkman, only so much as was enough for him to grab the bucket, fill it and hand it back. They were too shy even to face him, let alone speaking to him. And here we had a bunch of girls of in their early twenties, talking confidently in the presence of sixteen men; fifteen boys and Dr Saleh. Some girls were covered in long sheets to cover their bodies.

Boys were from various backgrounds. Some were local Lahorites, and some were from other parts of the Punjab. A small group from among the boys were dressed like advert models; very smart appearance, hinting that their interest in studies was going to be only secondary, if at all. Another group was dressed in flimsy trousers and oversized shirts. One could easily tell that it was their first time fitting themselves in the western-styled clothes; collar button was done but resting way below the collar bone, trousers very baggy and held up by the support of their belts. Their dress spoke out about the complexes they had brought with them. The group I fell into was wearing *shalwar-kamiz* suits. Some very neat and clean, others over-designed and a few over-starched to show pomp and power of their families back home in their villages. Mine was neat and clean but a fairly simple and straightforward one. Footwear again spoke a lot about those wearing it. I was wearing a pair of black Peshawari sandals: two straps of leather overlapping at the front with a buckle by the ankle. I had no shame in what I looked like. *I am what I am!* It was this very attitude that had distanced me from all bogus theories of life, including dogmatic belief.

I would only believe what convinced me and nothing more.

The introduction went on for more than the span of a lesson. This first day was nothing more introductions. We had lecturers walking into the lecture theatre, introducing themselves and all of us introducing ourselves again. This soon turned into a mechanical exercise beginning to give a stale taste. By break time, most of us were exceptionally bored except a few girls who could continue to chat for the rest of their lives. Most of the chatterboxes appeared to be from the lower middle class and seemed to know very well that this introduction was probably their only chance to capture a potential match or else they would have to live with a man of their parents' choice. This lot would happily get up, with a glowing face and introduce themselves as many times as they were asked; glancing at some guy of their choice who they believed was their god-made match.

I had no intention to get involved with girls simply because I knew Abbaji would only give me one single chance to qualify and wouldn't agree to bear any further costs for second or third attempts. I had no choice but to stay focused.

With the bell that rang to announce break time, we all walked our way to the university cafeteria. It was only a few corridors away but what a feeling it was to walk through the corridors where knowledge seemed to be flying in the breeze. But the cafeteria held a surprise for all of us. We thought universities had a fashion of free mixing but what we saw was quite the contrary. Men and women were segregated into two separate halls.

I grabbed a chair and drew it closer to a group of newcomers. We were supposed to know each other through the repeated introductions, but I still failed to put names to faces.

"Hey, Salik! Come, join us! Nice to meet you", said one of the guys who had been the most confident in the introductory sessions.

"*Asalamo Alaikum*", I said as I moved my chair closer their table.

"*Wa alaikum salam*", they all replied back.

For me, this prayer was only a way of saying Hello in Urdu. I didn't believe in the prayer it held. *Allah's Mercy on you.* I never believed that peace and mercy come from elsewhere. Call me a Buddhist, but I believed that peace comes from within and not without. While religion is easy to give up, culture is not. Culture runs in our blood. Even though I no longer believed in Allah, but I would still use the terms like *Insha-Allah* meaning *god willing* regarding any future plans I mentioned. These were the fragments of faith that have their roots in culture and run deep in your psyche, once you have been a believer.

The conversation over tea and *samosas* was all about girls; looks, bodies, smiles, laughs and anything to do with girls. However, I could not be a part of it. Why? I don't know. Maybe because I had decided once and for all that I would not play that league. But what shocked me and caught my attention was when the guys around the table started discussing the reason of girls being segregated. *A pressure group could be so strong that the University had to succumb to its demands and change their policy? The university administration had to build a separate hall so that the Jamiat could be happy?* This was unbelievable.

I had been brought up in a strictly religious household. I knew that a household in Islam is led by the father and the father was responsible for ensuring that everything in the household happened according to Islamic ritual. But I didn't know that the same could apply to a university. We had *Jamiat* to play the typical father-figure.

"Why? What's their problem?" I broke my silence.

Then there came all sorts of stories and gossip about the *Jamiat*. It was my first introduction to the pressure group called the *Jamiat-e-Talaba-e-Islam*, literally meaning the *Society of Students of Islam*, but actually meaning a bunch of thugs and henchmen.

Up to this point in my life, I hadn't believed in it, but I never hated Islam. I thought it was a matter of personal choice to believe or not to. But this was a turning point in my life as an atheist. I was now beginning to look at religion as a tool of force and coercion than only a way of life. As I got to know *Jamiat*, the seed of disgust for religion got sowed in my heart.

I was told that the *Jamiat* would not tolerate a boy and a girl together in the campus. Even if the couple said that they were brother and sister, they were still told to part ways while in the campus. Some boys, who had said on oath that they were nothing but a brother of the girl they were seen with were taken to a room in one of the hostels and tortured by pressing a piping hot iron on bare parts of their bodies. Lit cigarettes were pressed onto their private parts to punish them for being seen with a girl. Some were left so distressed that their helplessness had pushed them into depression, leaving them unable to pursue their education and careers.

This left me feeling extremely disgusted. *How could this be possible? Shouldn't this be a matter of personal choice? If a girl wants to be with a boy, just let her be. If Allah is unhappy with what she does, leave it for him to punish her when she gets to see him in the so-called hereafter.* On the one hand, they claim to have a prophet who they portray as a very loving man, and on the other, it's them, his followers, who seem to be the worst creatures on earth.

To hell with them! I moved on. I did not want to be sickened anymore. And my road wasn't going to cross theirs anyway because I wasn't here with any intention of pulling girls. So, I tried not to give this pressure group anymore thought.

The rest of the day was similar to the morning; more lecturers walking in, telling about themselves and trying to get to know us. I could bet they wouldn't remember even our names, not to speak of the lengthy introductions. For us, it was easy to remember the names of the lecturers and professors because there were only five of them. I could remember their names and the subjects they were going to teach us, but the one person who I could vividly remember was Dr Saleh. Maybe because he was the first one in that beautiful morning to walk into our class and introduce himself.

But perhaps there were other factors for me to have focused more on him than others. He was young and only a few years older than us. He was the only one to have done a PhD thesis on a serious topic from Reading University in England. The rest had acquired their PhDs from Punjab University or open universities on rundown topics like 'Iqbal and Politics', 'The Political Theory of Islam', 'The Political Structure of Medina' and 'Bhutto and his

Foreign Policy'. None of them interested me. But Dr Saleh had written his thesis on 'The Theocratic Foundations of the Islamic Republic of Pakistan'. This topic itself carried great irony. *Theocracy in a republic?* When he told us about his PhD research, I had for the first time in my life thought about a great contradiction that rested in the very name of my country. *The Islamic Republic of Pakistan. This is crazy!* I thought. *A state can either be Islamic or a Republic; there is no democracy in the Islamic political structure; it can't be both at the same time!*

It wouldn't be wrong to say that the very topic of Dr Saleh's thesis opened many avenues for my thought to tread upon. Almost everything in this 'Islamic Republic' was self-contradictory. Bhutto, supposedly the most liberal leader after Jinnah, too, was caught up in that unfortunate series of self-contradiction. He was a socialist but ended up twisting the socialist philosophy to be able to sell it to his Islamised nation. So, he coined the term 'Islamic Socialism'. *Sheer nonsense!* My list went on and on, and I felt ashamed to be part of a nation that was nothing but an ugly mixture of contradictions.

Thus, the very topic of his thesis had made Dr Saleh stand out in the rest of the teaching staff at the department.

CHAPTER SIX

Classes were now in full swing. Lecture after lecture and assignment after assignment took up most of my days and nights. It was great fun to be learning about what great minds had to say in their theories about political philosophy. I was introduced to the likes of Rousseau and Hobbes. I got to see how great minds had devoted their lives to exploring the structure of societies and how they were governed, ruled and controlled. They had done nothing but thought and reflected all their lives. *What a passion it must have been.*

Most of the names we would come across were of Western men. Gandhi, as an exception, was among the political philosophers we studied. There was not a single Pakistani to have made any contribution to this great discipline of knowledge. This alone was enough to tell why Pakistan had no political ideology. Jinnah was nowhere in the picture. Iqbal was forcefully pushed to be made a political philosopher, but he too had been an Indian all his life. And Iqbal was more of a tragedy than a fortune for Pakistan, as Pakistan had accepted him as the only one national hero and seemed to need no more. Same, unfortunately, is the case today.

He had been dragged in to perform roles he never claimed he could play. Poet and thinker were two titles he qualified for, but to be turned into a philosopher, a *Sufi*, a religious leader and, above all, a saint were the roles that got imposed on him long after his death by a society that had no role models. So, although there was a whole paper in the first year of my course on Iqbal's political thought, it never seemed to make sense to me because I never found him fit enough to be classified as a political philosopher.

I appreciated his efforts in Muslim awakening in the Indian subcontinent but never accepted him as the one who gave the vision of a Pakistan per se. He had demanded a state for the Muslims but as part of the *United States of India*, not as a cluster of states to be cut off and put aside as Pakistan. Calling Iqbal the birth-giver of the idea of Pakistan was one other contradiction in the so-called ideology of Pakistan.

Taking Iqbal out of the picture meant that there was no Pakistani philosopher among those that had shaped political philosophy as a discipline.

The more I got to know Iqbal, the more I got to realise that the whole idea of Pakistan was based on a pseudo-ideology of theocracy. Despite Jinnah having an extremely secular outlook, he too seemed to have fallen prey to the theocratic nature of the whole of Pakistan Movement. Pakistan was destined to eventually be ruled by the hardliner *mullahs* as theocracy was the basic ingredient of the ideology.

As I grew more and more curious to know where things went wrong with a Pakistan founded by the great men like M A Jinnah, Zafrullah Khan and Jogandar Nath Mandal, the more I became interested in knowing what conclusions Dr Saleh might have drawn in his doctoral thesis. The University of Reading had granted him a PhD, so it must have been a great work in the political history of Pakistan.

That gave me the courage to go knocking on his door one fine afternoon. His room was laden with books, folders, files, journals and anything to do with papers. All the paperwork was bulging out of shelves. Some books lay on his table and most of them on racks; some seemed old and others quite new. Some racks on the shelves had slightly curved from the centre, while others had succumbed to the weight. One shelf supported the other; otherwise, they would have collapsed. The biggest collection of books I had ever seen was the library of my college in Faisalabad, but the books in that tiny room alone outnumbered the whole collection of my college library.

"Good afternoon Salik! How can I help you?"

"Hello, Sir. Sorry to trouble you..."

"No, not a problem! It's never too much trouble to sit with one of my students. Talk to me!"

"Your thesis Sir... I've always wanted to read it. Could I... I mean if it's not too much trouble...?"

"Of course... you want to read it so you should. What stops you from doing so? I'm sure it's in the library. Have you checked there?"

"I have Sir, but it doesn't seem to be there. It's in the catalogue but not on the shelf..."

"O really? That's strange! Hmmm... O yeah! I remember. I got it issued and never returned it to the library. This bloody *Jamiat* can make a mountain of a molehill... a bunch of idiots... you know what they're like...they can't stand the truth... but you don't worry. I'll make it available for you. I might have a copy at home...if my wife hasn't joined hands with *Jamiat*."

Dr Saleh finished off his sentence with a loud laugh. He always did so. He would speak about the worst side of the Pakistani society and then laugh out loud. I enjoyed seeing him do this but failed to understand why he did so. While he left us scarred by a harsh fact about our society, he would burst into laughter.

This was my first actual introduction to Dr Saleh. He was a genuinely learned man. Him being so accommodating and welcoming to a young student who had literally just set foot in the university was very reassuring. He left me deeply inspired and ambitious that I too would take up higher research and produce something that could help my society discover its flaws and work towards fixing them.

Many days went by. Dr Saleh would come to our class, deliver his lecture, laugh and leave. I didn't have the courage to remind him that I was desperately waiting to have a glimpse of his thesis.

Finally, one day as he walked out of our classroom, he turned back and said,

"Salik, can you come upstairs to my room?"

I left my notebooks and my pens and pencils on my desk and dashed after him.

He had hardly made to his office that I was there standing behind him, waiting for him to open the door and walk into his office.

"Here you are, gentleman!"

Saying this, he held out a big, brown, heavy envelope to me.

"Oh, thank you, Sir. I won't take very long. I just need a few days…"

"Wonderful! That's impressive! It took me five long years to write this, and you will read it in only a few days… you sound to me like a genius… or a genie rather!"

Saying this, he burst into his usual laughter.

"No Sir, sorry Sir, what I meant was …"

"No need! I know what you mean… but this is a copy for you to keep. It took me days to dig out my thesis from thousands of books and bundles of papers scattered all over my study. Then I got it photocopied for you yesterday. I'm so happy that someone has actually approached me showing interest in my work. Please do keep it."

I was astonished. What a generous man! He actually got his thesis copied for me to keep. I felt honoured and humbled even by just holding a PhD thesis in my hands. It made me feel privileged to be even able to hold it, not to speak of having it for good.

"Are you sure, Sir?" I asked in my astonishment. This was too good to be true.

"Of course! It's for you to keep. I hope you find it useful."

I thanked him again. I must be glowing with thankfulness because I could see the reflection of that glow in his eyes. His eyes were shining as I had never before seen. He too seemed amazed, but wouldn't express it openly as I did. He had more experience of life than I did and knew how to stay composed.

As I rushed out of his room, he called me back "Salik, do you live in the hostel?"

"Yes Sir, I do."

"Oh! Ok! In that case, be careful. Don't leave it lying around, or you could be in trouble."

While I was absorbing this warning, he laughed out again. He always did this.

"Careful with what Sir?"

"Careful with *Jamiat*... They'll be on your case if they see you reading this type of material. I've quite openly criticised the very ideology of Pakistan. I've made bold claims that the theory of Pakistan as we know it today was never there in the time of Jinnah. This theory was coined later on to turn the state of Pakistan into a theocracy. A state where extremist hardliners could flourish religion as a business... But anyway... just take care... shouldn't be a problem if you keep it locked up in your cupboard!"

A cackle again... and I was out of his room.

The bundle that was already heavy felt even heavier. The burden of truth got added to the weight of paper. I was clutching it close to my body as I walked steadily towards my hostel. I was carrying it like a newborn baby as if I had given birth it. I was later to realise that it was I who had taken birth that day. This thesis of Dr Saleh was to give me a new life.

I did not sleep that night. I read on and on and just wouldn't stop. I just couldn't. The realisation that I had lived all my life with a false concept of the society was much more than only a shock to me. What we had read in the name of Pakistan's history was a white lie. My parents, my school teachers, my college lecturers, the Maulvi Sahib at the mosque all had lied to me all my life. Dr Saleh had told the truth in his thesis. Why every word of his seemed so believable was because he had given references to every claim. He had written nothing from himself; every line was very professionally referenced. This had opened up a whole new world of the power of academic research; the power of truth. This shifted my mind from the age old saying 'might is right', to the 'might of being right'. No statement was emotional. No claim was like a cliche. Yet every word spoke for itself of its truthfulness. I was spellbound and heartbroken at the same time. Spellbound by the truth I had discovered, heartbroken by the misinformation that I had been indoctrinated with.

I had never before come across Jinnah's speech to the first constituent assembly of Pakistan. He had guided them in clear-cut terms to draft a constitution where Muslims were free to go to their mosques, Hindus to their temples and Christians to their churches. He had asked for a constitution that deprived no one of religious rights. He had demanded to carve Pakistan's legislature into one where a Muslim seizes to be a Muslim, and a Hindu seizes to be a Hindu. Where everyone was above religious discrimination and where religion had nothing to do with the affairs of the state. I had never known this Jinnah. The Jinnah I had been introduced to all along was more of a Mullah who fought for a state where the rule of Islam would prevail.

Never before had I ever thought that if Pakistan was to be ruled by Islam, what brand of Islam would that be? The Islam of Maududi or the Barelvi Islam or the Shiite one? This question was an eye-opener for me. I had never imagined that my country was faced with multi-dimensional crises only and only in the attempt of turning it into an Islamic state.

With every paragraph, new questions kept popping up. Why was it that the Mullahs who called the concept of Pakistan as *Palidistan'*— or filthy land — during the freedom movement later migrated to Pakistan? Why did they later take the same *Palidistan* as their foster child and raise slogans like *'Pakistan ka Matlab kiya? La Ilaha Ilallah'* — Pakistan symbolises the One Allah? Dr Saleh had very rightly raised an absolutely valid question here. He had asked why such Mullahs are not held accountable for blasphemy when they take *Palidistan* and 'Allah' as synonymous?

Dr Saleh had held these hardliner Mullahs to be responsible for turning Pakistan into a chaos and failure. The same, he believed, were to be blamed for the terrorism that haunts the whole wide world.

I had kept my bedside light on all night. My roommates would grumpily utter sleepy complaints as they turned sides or as they got bit by a mosquito, but I had to read on. I knew that the intervals of complaining were short-lived as my roommates were in a deep sleep. I looked at their faces thinking how different one looks when asleep. Faces that glimmered all day look quite foolish when immersed in slumber. I smiled and carried on reading.

By the time the call for the morning prayer was sung in the university mosque, I had finished reading Dr Saleh's thesis. I got up and locked the thesis safely away in my cupboard. In the shower, I felt as if my old skin was getting washed away. Like a new, fresh skin was coming to surface. I felt like I had a new mind; like I was starting a new life today. With my heart, broke the model of Pakistan that was carved and placed on the mantle of my mind. It took a whole night for this old image to break. I hadn't made a new one yet. A whole new day and a whole new life lay ahead. I didn't want to rush in making a new model of my unfortunate homeland. Now it was my turn to develop the actual concept, and I was going take my time!

CHAPTER SEVEN

S o far, I had successfully managed to refrain from being carried away by what had swept most of the other guys: girls! I had been successful so far in keeping my focused on studies. One needs a vent, but I believed that girls could not fill the void. None of the girls in my class seemed to have the intellectual capacity that could provide me with a vent if I ever had to go down this way to look for one. There was a handful who got very good marks in tests and assignments, but that reflected not their intellectual calibre but their capacity to memorise. The educational system in Pakistan is all about having a good memory. The more you can rote learn, the higher the chances of securing good marks. This remains one of the tragedies of the decaying society. Most universities enrolled students on merit, but merit did *not* mean merit in the strictest sense of the word. It merely meant good grades in exams with the high achievers making it to the so-called top universities. Exams were all written, and no other form of assessment was carried out to test the depth of knowledge and its understanding. Thus, many of those who managed to get into universities for higher education were the ones who had committed their syllabi to memory. Some of them would be bright enough to understand what they had memorised, but the majority owed it to their memory. It was the same lot that made their way into the civil service, hence shaping a bureaucracy that was as ignorant as the ruling class, if not worse.

I never really had the chance to brag about my memorising skills because I 'wasted' most of my time trying to understand and grasp what I had read. I could not move on unless I felt that I had gained a grasp of the idea. This, as always, left me to fall somewhere in the mediocre or slightly below-average band of my class as far as grades were concerned.

Thus, no girl had attracted my attention so far. But something strange happened one day. Shamaila, the girl from Kinnaird, caught me gawking at her. She passed a smile, but it went unnoticed. She then waved to try and catch my eye, and that startled me. I must have looked extremely cheap starting at her in a gaze not even knowing she had noticed. I quickly waved back with a nervous smile and shifted my gaze back to the board where Mrs Inayat was explaining how the church ruled every section of the society in Medieval Europe.

It might not have been that bad, but I believed that gawking at girls was not very gentleman-like. I wished I could tell her that it wasn't her I was staring at. What had caught my attention and held it there for so long wasn't her appearance. It was her earrings. They were the exact same as my mother would always wear. Small baskets facing downwards with tiny beads hanging at the edges. I knew that they were called *jhumkay*. I knew this word from my very childhood. I could recall holding on to them as Ammi would put me to sleep. I would clutch onto it as she complained that it hurt but I couldn't help it. It was an obsession. I had to hold on to them to fall asleep.

"Let go!" She would say with a borderline tone of love and anger.

She would hug me when I came home from playing with other children in the playground. I was very young, and she would have to sit down to hug me. The *jhumkas* always brushed my forehead as I would rest my head on her shoulder.

She would be kneading the dough for *chapatis*, and her *jhumkas* would swing from her ears like a pendulum.

Those pendulums would swing even as she rocked on a small wooden stool while washing the laundry.

As my eyes caught sight of Shamaila's *jhumkas*, I slipped back into a nice, warm and bright flashback of my childhood. Every scene to do with those *jhumkas* flickered like a film before my eyes. I could still smell my mother's sweat that I would sense as she lay next to me.

I wanted to tell Shamaila that I was not the type of guy that would stare at girls. I wanted to tell her why my gaze was fixed on her. But I couldn't. I feared to reveal the child in me if I did tell her the truth.

Fortunately or unfortunately, she took it as a signal. My waving back in embarrassment worked as the cherry on the cake. She was convinced that I was interested. This led to the first advance that she made towards me. Maybe she wanted to make a move anyway, but Pakistani girls do not take the lead in expressing an interest. They wait or even create a situation, where the boy expresses interest, and they pretend to just follow innocently. As if they were obliging the boy by responding positively to his advancing steps.

"I was wondering if you had notes on Rawl's concept of justice."

This was the opening line of the first ever dialogue we were going to have. I knew she wasn't actually after my notes on Rawl. It was rather only an attempt to make the take-off as smooth as possible. I couldn't ruin her attempt. I was taught to be nice and kind to people. Then, after all, I was a man.

"Yes, I think I do. Why?"

"What do you mean why?" She chuckled, "Because I need them. I'll get them copied. So, can I borrow them?" She talked as if we had known each other for a long time.

Smiling back, I could only say, "Of course you can. Why not? Here you go!"

She grabbed them and went back to the small group of girls that stood waiting for her. Joining them, she said something that I missed. All I heard was a congregation of giggles, which was a bit curious and embarrassing. *What was that all about?* They seemed to be making a fool of me. It was probably my first experience of talking to a girl who wasn't a cousin. This alone was a strange experience, let alone the seeming mockery at the hand of a bunch of girls. I felt foolish but didn't give it much thought. I had soon moved on, and all I was worried about was getting my notes back safely.

A few days passed by with no sign of my notes being returned. Perhaps she wanted me to approach her and ask to kindly return my notes. I didn't want to do this. I like to think that it was only masculine ego that stopped me from doing so, but in my heart, I knew I was just too shy to approach her. She was a larger-than-life kind of character. She was dropped off and picked up by a driver, she wore nice, light coloured, tight cotton trousers. Her blouse would be loosely fitted with colours of summer fruits and big floral designs. She would lift up her file to an angle where the bright sun couldn't get to her fair complexion. She wore Ray-Ban shades that she would remove while stepping into the corridor that led straight to our department. No makeup, just a very light pink lip-gloss, only to enhance the natural colour of her lips.

Anyone could tell she was from a wealthy family. What had made me think about her was not her beauty but the fact that she would arrive sitting in the backseat of a car. A driver would open the door for her, and she would strut straight to the corridor. I had associated that lifestyle with people of very high status like ministers and ambassadors. A girl in her twenties doing all that was a strange sight.

I had hardly ever thought about her as only just a girl. Never as a beautiful one. I had never pictured her the way boys would usually picture girls to satisfy their desires. But I must say that I had thought about her on occasions. Her image had only been of a powerful and dominating personality. What her home looked like, the servants and maids they had, the great post her father worked at, were the only things that came to mind about her. My imagination of Shamaila had been nothing more than her social status.

I felt overawed by her confidence. I never knew one could laugh with such rich passion in a society that was falling apart; a society full of sorrows; a society without a future; a society with no vision.

I would sometimes think that she too was visionless, or else she wouldn't be so cheerful. But she wasn't visionless. She was the only one girl in the whole of the class who spoke with conviction. She was the only one to have raised issues in class that weren't shallow. She sounded like a Marxist when she got the chance to speak about the ever-widening gulf between the rich and the poor. But that made her look like a hypocrite. How could a girl driven every day to the university by a chauffeur in a big saloon car have the audacity to question the unequal distribution of wealth? The only conclusion, if any, was that she was but blindly following a fashionable trend. She knew that raising issues of the underprivileged classes of society could earn easy popularity. Then again, she had good control over her choice of words that made her capable of delivering with conviction.

One morning, as I walked on the scenic route along the canal from my hostel to the department, her car drove past. The department was only a mere hundred yards away. The brake lights came on as the car steadily swerved off the main road. By the time I got to the corridor of our department, she had got out of her car. Her driver was getting back in his seat to drive off. She stopped halfway through the corridor and looked for something in her bag. I got off the walkway onto the grass belt that ran along the corridor. I didn't want to bump into her so, I tried to stay away. As I walked parallel to the corridor on the grass belt, I could see from the corner of my eye that I had walked past and left her behind. But she was out and loud.

"Hey Salik, don't you want your notes back?"

I stopped and turned around

"Yeah. Have you got them?"

"What if I told you I lost them?"

What would I do? I asked myself, so I could put together a reply.

"Erm... I would prepare them again I suppose?"

"Really? You wouldn't complain? You wouldn't have a go at me?"

"No."

"Gosh, you're so boring," she said, laughing.

"Anyway, here you go!" She pulled out my notes and slammed them on my spread-out hand

"Excuse the doodling. It's a bad habit. See you later."

As if it was her birthright to do anything to someone else's property! As if I should have been thankful for the doodling on my notes! I looked at my notes to see what she had made of them. The very first page had my name written on it. *Salik*. It was written in a feminine handwriting, the *i* with a smiley face on top. It seemed to be more like a henna tattoo design. Then, next to my name was a cartoon face. Nose, eyes and ears like Mickey Mouse but hair done neatly with a parting on the side, just as I did my hair. The doodling hadn't done any harm to the notes as such, so I didn't care too much about it, just that I liked to keep my notes and notebooks tidy.

The day went on as normal. Even if you enjoy your subject, a monotonous routine of study can make it a bit dull at times. I had this boredom surround me on that lazy day. I was desperate to get back to my room as soon as classes were over. I grabbed my books and rushed back. I didn't want to be distracted because I knew I would get carried away with any chitchat. All I wanted was a good nap. I had stayed up all night reading Dr Saleh's thesis. I had checked up on him a couple of times during the day, but he wasn't around. I was told he was attending a conference for the next three days and wouldn't be back until early next week. Had he been there, I would have gone and told him how his thesis had captivated me and how it had been an eye-opener. I wanted to share the feeling, but there seemed to be no one who could share the burden. The burden of truth that comes with enlightenment.

I had walked out of the corridor without being distracted. I was too focused on making it to the hostel and to fall on my bed when a car pulled up right in front of me, freezing me in my steps. The tinted glass of the rear window slid down but only halfway. *Stuck-up snob!* I thought as Shamaila's eyes appeared from behind the half-open window.

"Salik! I didn't manage to get your notes copied. I read them but was wondering …"

"Wondering what?" I asked, cutting her halfway

"… wondering if I could borrow them again and have them copied today. You can come and get them from my place. Just straight down, along the canal. You'll see a board saying 'Bahria Colony' on the left. Drive off that road and …"

"It's alright," I cut in again. "Here you go. Bring it back tomorrow. I don't think I need it tonight". That was quite out of order. Sitting in her car, the window only halfway down and guiding me to her house. She knew that I didn't have a car that I could drive off the main road to get to her villa in Bahria Colony. I handed her the stack of notes and walked off. I thought it was fine not to say anymore or to exchange formal Hi's and Byes to such a brat.

CHAPTER EIGHT

The coach took forever to get to Faisalabad. The road was in tatters, with road works every few miles. I wanted to get to Faisalabad as soon as I could. I hadn't been able to think right since I received the phone call the previous night.

Abbaji had told me off as soon as I got to the receiver and held it to my ear.

"I've been trying to get hold of you for the last three hours! Why does your hostel phone stay engaged?"

"Abbaji, there are around a hundred and eighty men living in this hostel. They all get phone calls. The phone stays busy. I'm sorry."

I couldn't tell him that boys in the hostel got long calls from their girlfriends. I was one of the few who had no girlfriend and hence this was the first ever time I was talking on this telephone handset which was fixed on the wall of the lobby. Had I told him the reality, he might have told me to leave such a 'shameless place' and forget about studying any further. So I had to lie.

"Whatever! Look, your mother is in hospital. She had a heart attack this morning. She wants to see you."

It was almost One O'clock at night. I stuffed my bag with a few clothes and dashed to the main road with the hope to be able to catch a late night bus to the coach station. There was no public transport whatsoever. It was around two o'clock when I decided to walk to the bridge right at the end of the campus. But when I got there, I saw that no buses were running so I caught a rickshaw and asked the driver to rush me to the coach station.

"Is everything alright, Sir Ji?" It's very common in Pakistan to break the ice and start a conversation with a stranger. Rickshaw drivers, taxi drivers and barbers have the habit of doing so. Surprisingly, no one really minds such personal questions, and neither did I.

"Not really. My mother is in hospital in Faisalabad. I need to go and see her."

"Don't worry. God willing, she'll be fine. What happened to her?"

His questions were coming in reverse order, but I knew that for him it was only a habitual conversation. It didn't have to have substance. I told him what had happened to her.

"Heart attacks are becoming too common! You see, when there is nothing pure to eat, what else can you expect? Everything's contaminated. There's so much pollution. Buses and trucks puffing out so much fume and smoke. Even my own rickshaw. I had it fixed but ended up spending two thousand rupees for that."

He could've gone on and on. Thanks to the empty roads that we reached the coach station quickly and the conversation pretty much ended there. From my mother's heart attack to the repair costs of a rickshaw; I wonder what would have come next.

"How much?" I asked getting out of the rickshaw.

"Just a hundred, Sir Ji."

I didn't have the courage to haggle, so I handed him a hundred rupees and grabbed my things to catch the first coach to Faisalabad.

I had only just turned to rush when I heard the rickshaw driver calling out,

"Sir Ji! Here, keep twenty rupees. Your mother is ill. Give it to charity. Allah give her health!"

"No, it's fine," I shouted back. "Get something nice for your kids."

"I can't! I've already set it aside for charity. I can't use it for my kids, Sir Ji!"

I had to go back and get it from him.

"Thank you!"

That's all I could say. I felt compelled to respect the poor man's dogmatic generosity.

"No problem, Sir Ji! Allah bless your mother with health. I'll ask my wife to pray for her. Her prayers are always heard. *Salam!*"

I was touched. *I can't believe there are still people like this who care for others.* A hundred rupees was already very reasonable for the journey, and he had given back twenty for me to give in alms. I didn't believe in alms and prayers, but his sentiments could not be ignored. Religion can work wonders. While it may help raise terrorists, it can reinstate a level of humanity in society. I managed to catch the very early morning coach. But I couldn't stop thinking about the driver and his act of sympathy.

I thought that the society that I lived in was not as disappointing as I had always seen it to be. There were still good persons who could bring about change. But the chain of corruption runs from top to bottom and not the other way. I was being pessimistic again. But then there were people like Dr

Saleh who could influence the top brass of the society, but he too was afraid of having his works getting into the hands of *Jamiat*. By the time I got off the coach in front of Allied Hospital in Faisalabad, I had reached strange conclusions. To be a decent person in society, one has to either be a PhD like Dr Saleh or be completely ignorant and poor like the rickshaw driver. The in-between class is where the nucleus of a corrupted society flourishes.

I reached the hospital and waited for the lift, but it seemed to take forever. I took the five flights of stairs up to the ward where Ammi was admitted.

She had a mask of oxygen on but was fully conscious. She saw me and tried to get up, but I rushed to her to save the hassle, so she stayed where she was. She held on to me as her tears streamed down her cheeks.

"Ammi, what's this? Save the drama! You should've just told me to come?"

I tried to make a joke out of the situation. I knew that what would be bothering her right now was not her health but the fact that I had to travel in a state of worry. I cracked another couple of jokes, which helped to calm the situation.

"Shall I get you some fruit?" I asked

"No. You stay put. I've already disturbed your studies. But you can go back when you want to. I just wanted to see you. I'll be fine!"

This woman, my mother, whose literacy level was next to nothing was so concerned about my education. I wanted to hug her again but I couldn't. I was a fully grown man. I felt too shy doing so, so I just stood by her bedside. I didn't want to leave her, but I knew I had to. I loved her so much, but I had always been bad at expressing emotion. I thought I should move away or I might break down. I made an excuse that I had to make a phone call to let my department know that I would not be attending university for the next few days.

I walked out of the ward and went down the stairs to the marketplace just by the gates of the hospital. I wanted to do something for Ammi, but there wasn't much I could do except buy her some fruit. I got half a dozen apples from one of the vendors. He asked for eighty rupees. I had only sixty in my pocket, so I asked him to take one out. But then I remembered the twenty rupees that the rickshaw driver had given me back.

"It's alright. I'll take six," I told the vendor.

He, in return, handed me back the bag of six apples.

As I took the bag, it flashed to my mind that the twenty rupees were meant to be for charity. *So what!* I brushed off the thought. I didn't believe in all this. But I felt as if the twenty rupee note was no longer mine. I felt overwhelmed by superstition. *It's fine!* I tried to convince myself. But something inside me stopped me from buying my ailing mother apples with the twenty rupees that the driver had dedicated for alms. *He didn't want to spend it on his children, so why should I do it on my mother.* I went back to the vendor and asked him to take an apple or two out of the bag and give me twenty rupees back.

"What happened? They're juicy and sweet! Take them all."

"I forgot I needed twenty rupees, I don't have any more cash", I said in a dry tone to avoid this conversation dragging on. He murmured with a cross face, took two apples out and almost threw a twenty rupee note back at me. I picked it up and walked back towards the stairs. I looked around and saw beggars sitting in a line against a wall. I approached the first beggar in the line and handed him the twenty rupees. He looked at my face in astonishment. Then he looked carefully at the note, probably to check that it wasn't fake. He lifted his hand holding the note to his forehead to thank me and said many prayers in return. I left him chanting prayers, that he had been giving to almost everyone all day, and made my way to the ward.

Ammi was surrounded by a team of doctors. I went closer and asked how she was doing. The duty doctor explained to me that the attack was minor and that medication alone should help her recover.

No surgical procedures were required at this stage, but it was essential that she changed her lifestyle; took less stress, ate more fruit and vegetables, avoided red meat, exercised more and tried to remain positive.

I sat with Ammi in the back seat of the taxi while Abbaji took the front seat. The front seat is a symbol of honour in Pakistani society, and all honour and praise belong to a father, the demi-god. So he was where he belonged. I was thinking of how I could tell the doctors that my mother's lifestyle could not be changed. She's a typical Pakistani woman. She had been shaped from her very childhood to be what she was, with no choice of her own. Abbaji would tell her what was best for her and he had already told her that red meat wasn't harmful.

"These doctors chat rubbish sometimes. How can you gain your energy back if you have no meat? Nonsense! I'll get you some mutton tomorrow. Make soup out of it and have the meat with rice. You should be fine!"

That was his verdict, and Ammi seemed to fully agree. I couldn't say much. I might have been doing a master's degree, but then Abbaji's qualification was being the head of the family.

I stayed in the *Haweli* for a couple of days. Ammi was recovering from her weakness, breathlessness and body ache that the heart attack had left behind.

Then, on the third morning after her release from the hospital, as I came out of the shower, she called me to the kitchen and told me that breakfast was ready.

"What on earth are you doing here, Ammi?"

"I'm fine! I can't sit idle. I can't tell you how much I missed making *paratha*s for you in the morning. Now come on, eat up. You don't want them to get cold."

The *paratha*s had the same crunch and taste. I had been to quite a few famous food stalls in Lahore with friends. There was a wide range of foods, but nothing quite touched the spot like Ammi's *paratha*s.

I started chomping on the *paratha* that had just come off the pan. Ammi was rolling another one out. As she rolled the pin, I noticed her *jhumkas* dangling, as always.

Ammi and I talked for a whole hour at breakfast. She had fried one *paratha* for herself in butter which she thought was better than processed oil. I would tell her it wasn't, but that too was like her belief in god. She believed so, and Abbaji endorsed the belief, so she wasn't ready to give it a second thought. She was the only one in the family who had asked me how I was doing in studies. I told her about the wealthy and modern girl who wore *jhumkas* like her; the *jhumkas* that didn't go with the rest of her outfit, but she wore them regardless. Ammi smiled and looked at me with a bit of curiosity as I talked about Shamaila and I had to clarify that all I knew about her was that she wore *jhumkas* and nothing more.

Wrapping up the breakfast table, Ammi said, "Salik *beta,* you ought to go back now. I've done enough harm to your studies. I'm perfectly fit. Don't waste any more time. Catch a bus today and go back."

"Are you sure?" I asked.

And she was absolutely sure. Abbaji walked in wiping his hands with a towel, all ready for breakfast.

"When are you planning to go back?"

"Maybe today!"

"It's best that you go back now. We've paid the fees for the whole year. Quite a few days wasted already. Your mother is better now."

They both wanted me to go back, but for different reasons.

It was very gracious and merciful of Abbaji to give me a lift to the coach station. On our way, there was little exchange of conversation. I asked about his business, and he complained as usual. He asked how long my course would take and I told him that I had another eighteen months to go. I gave him the reassurance that fees would not be due for another six months.

"Do you say *namaz* on time?"

I stayed quiet as if I hadn't heard him in the traffic that roared too loud. My grip grew stronger on my bag.

"Do you offer *namaz* on time, regularly?"

This came louder and with an addition. I didn't want it to get any louder and any more explicit.

"Yes Abbaji, I do," I lied.

On the coach, I thought about the *haweli* and how it had all changed and how I had felt completely estranged to it. How I had become estranged to not only the *haweli* but the whole of the town called Faisalabad. I also thought about the rickshaw driver who had dropped me off at the coach station a few nights ago. I really wished to tell him that I had given the money in alms, and also that Ammi had survived the heart attack and was doing remarkably well now. How happy he would be to know that his wife's prayers had been answered, yet again. *Poor guy!*

CHAPTER NINE

It was almost midnight when I arrived back at the hostel. I went straight to my room where Akhtar was still awake and reading a book in the dim light of his bedside lamp.

"*Asalamo Alaikum*"

"*Wa alaikum salam*"

He got up and embraced me. Hugging is a customary way of showing affection in Muslim society. He showed his concern and asked about Ammi. One of the few things I still liked about the Pakistani society was the concern people generally had for those around them. We had a short chat about how things had been. I told him that I hadn't eaten for hours and was terribly hungry.

"Let's go out and have dinner. I haven't eaten too. Didn't feel like it, but I'm hungry now".

We walked down the stairs and turned towards the food stalls. The hostels and food kiosks were buzzing with life. Students, hundreds of miles away from their homes, were feeding themselves. They all must have mothers at home who must be missing them like my mother missed me. I knew that while there were many factors that gave my mother a heart attack, one factor was her concern that she had harboured ever since I had left the *haweli* and stayed away from home for such a long time.

The whole area was lit up with lights that shone in and around the food kiosks. Everyone seemed happy. All you could hear was chatter and laughter. Campus life was at its height. That was all very comforting. I had gradually started taking the university and the hostel as my second home. I was fully a part of it now. It was that moment when I realised that I had fallen in love with this new phase of my life.

I told Akhtar about the rickshaw driver. I told him about his conviction in prayer and how he had given me back twenty rupees to give away in alms. I could see a glow on Akhtar's face. I had always thought that Akhtar too was not a believer. When everyone would rush off to the mosque at the call to prayer from the mosque, Akhtar would either stay in the room or just wander off in a direction other than that of the mosque. I wanted to have a like-minded friend. I had always wanted to ask him so he could come out and declare it at least to me. But I knew that I would have to proclaim my disbelief before he did. One of us had to be the first drop.

As we started to eat, an interval fell in our conversation. I broke the silence with an irrelevant question.

"Akhtar, do you believe in prayers being answered?"

I saw Akhtar's face go slightly pale. The smile that had been on his face when he had listened to the rickshaw driver incident, vanished.

Uh-oh! I had touched the wrong cord.

"You don't have to answer! It's fine. I just asked. It's fine."

I knew it wasn't fine. I now knew that he never believed in religion and its paraphernalia, but had never been encountered so boldly on this matter.

"It's fine Akhtar! Carry on eating. The food is really nice."

I was trying to undo what I had just done. I wanted to lighten the mood.

"This *Daal Chawal* is really tasty, isn't it?"

"It is," Akhtar replied briefly.

He answered many of my questions that I asked to drive his attention away from what I had asked earlier very bluntly. All of his replies had now become short and crisp. This wasn't Akhtar. He was a student of philosophy and was very fond of philosophising any issue that got touched upon, even if it was just a passing statement.

I thought I should pay the bill as a price for what I had done, so I did. We walked back to the hostel. As we stepped onto the staircase, I said,

"Akhtar, I'm sorry! I shouldn't have asked..."

Akhtar got even more agitated. He started looking around and signalled me to stay quiet.

"Let's go to our room and talk," he whispered as he briskly walked up the stairs.

This was strange. I followed him trying to keep pace with his brisk steps. I stayed quiet until we reached our room. Akhtar seemed disturbed, and I was worried about what could have gone wrong. Then I said something to try and calm Akhtar down,

"Akhtar, you don't need to worry. I also don't believe in religion. I don't believe in prayer and all that. Take it easy. I won't do any harm!"

Akhtar simply ignored my bold proclamation. He only whispered, looking stealthily at Salim who was fast asleep.

"Why did you ask?"

I was totally confused. I could only apologise.

"I'm so sorry Akhtar! I know I shouldn't have. It just slipped out. It's just one of those stupid mistakes we all make at times. I know it's a private matter but ..."

"No! You don't need to be sorry. Did you just ask or were you told to ask?"

"No Akhtar, no one told me to ask. I just asked. Because I don't believe in all this! I thought I might find someone like minded..."

He seemed slightly relaxed. He sat on the bed, with his head down. He seemed to have come out of a fit. I didn't know what to do, but my silence could have seemed hostile in this situation.

I wanted to say something, but Akhtar spoke out, sounding much relaxed,

"I hope you understand how this *Jamiat* thing works. You never know who might be spying on you..."

"No, no! It's fine. It's okay. Don't worry. I know how sensitive this can get. I should've been more sensible. Let's go to sleep. We've got classes tomorrow."

We went to bed, but I couldn't go to sleep. Akhtar's reaction to my question had left me in shock. I couldn't get my head round the nervousness and distress that he had shown on my question. I knew for sure that he didn't believe, but the fact that he reacted so strangely to it was a puzzle that I couldn't solve.

The call to prayer from the central mosque in the campus was loud enough to wake anyone up, even if it wasn't for the likes of myself. The *Azan* woke me up quite early. My lectures on a Tuesday started at around 10.30, so I had planned to sleep or just lay in bed that morning, but once the prayer-call woke me up, I couldn't get to fulfil that desire. I decided to stay in bed and just enjoy the sluggishness I was drenched in. I hid my head under the covers, but I knew that Akhtar woke up with the prayer-call and made his way to the bathroom. That is what he did every single morning, but what always remained a mystery to me was that I never saw him go to the mosque. I would wake up but sink under the covers pretending to be asleep because I didn't have to go to the mosque. Akhtar would always wake up and make his way to the bathrooms and then disappear for half an hour or so. But that day, I had come to know that he did so to avoid *Jamiat* nagging him for not attending the prayer.

I had been approached by *Jamiat* guys on a couple of occasions. They would knock on my door, greet me with the utmost respect, enter the room uninvited and sit on my bed or on the chairs in the room. Then they would give me a sermon on the importance of prayer and that I was hell-bound if I didn't take *namaz* seriously.

"*Bhai*, be careful with prayers. We don't want to take action. We hope you have understood and you'll now attend the mosque five times a day. *Salam!*"

"*Salam!*" I replied as I shut the door. *Idiots!* I would say slamming the door shut. I didn't pay heed, and nothing really happened.

But Akhtar, I thought, was not as brave may be. He didn't want even this much of an encounter with *Jamiat,* so he decided to live a pretentious life as long as he was on the campus.

Salim was still as fast asleep as he had been when Akhtar and I had come back from dinner after last night's episode. He always slept like a baby. He had the stamina to sleep for the entire day and night.

As the door squeaked, and Akhtar walked in, it was almost daybreak, but blanket hanging on our window worked well to keep the light out. Very dim daylight came through the thick blanket we used to hang in place of a curtain to keep the daylight out. I saw Akhtar's silhouette walking to his cupboard, taking something out of his pocket, putting it in one of the drawers of the closet, shutting the cupboard and get back in his bed.

"*Salam,* Akhtar!"

"*Salam.* How are you?"

"I'm good, and you?" I said reluctantly. I felt nervous talking to him. I didn't want to trigger a panic attack by saying something wrong. But Akhtar sounded quite normal.

"I'm fine," he said. "Up for an early breakfast?"

I wanted to stay in bed, but I didn't know what might happen if I declined.

"Yeah, sure. Let's go. I'll quickly have a shower" I said, dreadfully adding the tag "…if ..that's.. alright..?"

"Yeah sure, go on. I'm ready and waiting."

I rushed to the showers. I wanted to be with Akhtar in a hope to see if he revealed any more about last night. I knew I wasn't going to ask, but I also knew that Akhtar was really embarrassed about the previous night's episode. We got along very well and always had a good chat when we got the chance to be together, but this offer for breakfast was unusual. I had a feeling that he now somehow wanted to make up for yesterday's reaction. I knew how awkward he must be feeling!

There was a mess in every hostel where all three meals were served daily, but Akhtar insisted that he wanted to treat me to a full cooked breakfast in the main cafeteria. Everything was as normal as it had always been before the previous night. I was happy because I was relieved of the feeling that I had hurt Akhtar and pushed him into a panic attack. He sounded even more friendly and open towards me. We talked about all sorts of things as we waited for breakfast to be served. Everyone seemed to be in a rush. Some were reading, others were preparing for a test or assessment as they hurriedly sipped their teas. I was lucky to be starting late that day, so I could take it easy. I didn't ask Akhtar why he wasn't in a rush, but it seemed that the breakfast and the 'meeting' he wanted to have with me over breakfast were more important to him than anything else.

"I hear you are seen with the top girl of your class..."

Akhtar took me by surprise.

"What girl?" I asked before he even finished his question.

"The daughter of Jalal Ali. I don't know her name, but everyone knows her father is the director of Lahore horticulture department."

"Shamaila?" I asked secretively. I sounded ignorant as I asked. Akhtar from another department happened to know about her family background, and I didn't.

"I don't know her name. All I heard was that you've been seen with her. But make sure that you don't get seen by *Jamiat*. If I can know this, I am sure JTI also know by now. Be careful!"

I told him that it was nothing more than her borrowing my notes and returning them to me. But my mind went numb with the realisation that rumours took no time to spread around the campus. I didn't really care much about *Jamiat* booking me and torturing me with lit cigarettes and steam irons. I had nothing to do with that girl, and even if I did, I wouldn't be scared of nonsensical mullahs.

This came and passed. We had finished our breakfast, but we had another set of tea to get a kick start for the day. We had hit a point where pauses of silence started to get longer. I had a sense of guilt from the night before, so I felt it my duty to break every pause of silence and crack a conversation.

"Akhtar, I would never have thought they taught Philosophy in Chiniot."

I asked with a broad smile so Akhtar could know it was nothing more than a light-hearted comment.

But Akhtar's smile vanished. *Bloody hell! I've hit another wrong cord!!!*

"I mean ... What I meant was ... WHAT IS SO WRONG WITH EVERYTHING I ASK?" I exclaimed as I tried to suss the mess I had made.

"Salik, I've been thinking all night, and I need to share something with you. I am not from Chiniot. I am from a small town near Chiniot."

"Ok? Then why did you say you were from Chiniot?"

"I just had to. And what I'm going to tell you now remains between you and me..."

"Sure. That's a deal! Don't worry. Go on!" I emphasised so much so he could know that I meant what I said. He wanted reassurance before he could tell me the strangest truth I had ever heard.

CHAPTER TEN

I had been away from the campus for four days only,
but it seemed it like I had been gone for years. As
I got ready to head to the department, I could still
feel the spices churning in my stomach from the desi
style omelette we had had. I felt bloated. It wasn't
only my stomach, my heart too felt quite heavy, bur-
dened with a truth that had just come to surface.
Akhtar had told me a story that was strange and
hard to digest. I had a sceptic mind, so I still had to
sieve fact from fiction. What he said could not be all
true. I had judged that he was paranoid so it could
well be that he was magnifying some of the points.

I got out of the hostel and turned right to head to the walkway that ran along the canal. I had missed that beautiful walk all those days. The food stall vendors were washing and cleaning their stalls to get them ready before the hostelites started to flood in by afternoon. That was the only time they could do the cleaning because, during the mornings, everyone took to the canteens and cafeterias on the other side of the canal, closer to their departments.

"*Salam,* Salik *Saab!*" Shouted Rafiq, the *Daal Chawal* guy of whom I was a regular customer.

"*Salam!*" I shouted back. His *Salam* had sent a wave of homely feeling down my body. The campus had become my home. I loved being here and hardly ever missed the *haweli.* I did miss Ammi, but the phases would come and go in seconds. Taking my clothes to the launderette, having breakfast on my own, seeing the kitchen staff in the hostel kneading dough for *chapatis,* going to bed at night and having no one to say good night in a warm, motherly tone. All such occasions would make me miss Ammi, but then there was so much going on in life, that I could hardly stop by such memories and pamper them. I would move on quickly, and Ammi's memories would fly back to the *haweli,* far away in Faisalabad. Very far from Lahore. *Ammi must have wrapped up the breakfast session and must be filling up the bucket to wash the whole courtyard of the haweli with the broom that had stiff, spiky straws.* I had only got to hear one or two strokes of the broom that I had already got off the walkway along the canal on the grassy plot that led to the corridor of my department.

The corridor looked like a still life painting from the angle I saw it that day. The columns and pillars all lined up in perspective; light passing through them to make a zebra-crossing pattern of light and shade on the floor of the corridor, punctuated by the colourfully dressed students that rushed through the corridor to make it in time for their lectures.

"Salik!" Shamaila shouted from behind.

I stopped, looked back and waited for her to come nearer. But she was too fond of being loud. She kept on shouting. As she approached me, she asked,

"Where have you been? I thought you were dead …"

She laughed as she walked briskly towards me. I gave her an abridged version of the long story of Ammi's heart-attack. She didn't look sad. She remained full of life.

"You should have stayed longer, idiot. The department won't shut down without you! And, by the way, you didn't even bother to tell anyone that you were going."

"I did. I told my roommate to inform Ghulam Rasool in the office."

"Nice! So you actually expected Ghulam Rasool to come looking for me and tell me, *Madam, Lord Salik has gone back to his village in an emergency.*"

"It's not a village Shamaila! It's the biggest industrial city in the whole of Punjab. And why should I have to tell you?"

"Yeah! Why would you tell me? Why should I have thought so? True, very true."

Everything she said would always be full of sarcasm. Nothing could brush away her jolly mood. She just laughed it off and entered the lecture room.

She was seated in front of me. Her hair was tied in a bun, and I could see her neck. A beautiful neck guarded by two golden *jhumkas*, rocking with every slight movement of her head.

I was looking at the world through her earrings when she turned around and startled me.

"Give me a pen, quickly."

She said in a very commanding tone as her pen gave up halfway through the lecture. I was trying to find one in my side pocket when she leant back and snatched the pen I was writing with.

"Quick!"

Bloody hell! What kind of a girl is she? She would have hit me if I hadn't given her my pen. I couldn't find an extra pen in my pocket, so I sat listening to the lecture, not taking any notes.

Mrs Inayat paused to pull out a new set of slides out of her bag. There was silence. Shamaila turned around again.

"Now what?" I asked crossly.

She just laughed cheekily, "Why aren't you writing? Always carry extra pens. You never know when you might need one!"

"Thanks for the tip!"

"Don't worry, you can have my notes later. Copy them and give them back to me."

"Can I have my own notes first, the ones you borrowed twice and have forgotten all about them!"

"Oh yeah! Tomorrow, definitely tomorrow. I've got them copied. I didn't know you were coming back. I thought you were dead!"

How could she be buzzing with joy all the time? Doesn't she have anything at all to worry about? Does money actually take away all your sorrows? Does wealth make you so confident that you take everything in the world to be your property? Does one have to be born to a bureaucrat family to be so carefree? Do you become powerful merely if your parents are at a high rank in the establishment?

I was caught up with all these reflections in a beautiful summer morning. Sunlight shone through the large windows, up above the high walls of the lecture room. The shadow of the tall branches of oak trees waved and disrupted the sunlight from fully embracing the ceiling.

I was getting ready for another burst of teaser-trailers of this girl to come my way after the lesson. I knew something would come as soon as the class ended. But when the class did end, she almost threw my pen back at me and rushed after the group of girls who were now off to the canteen. She didn't even say a word. *But why should she? Why was I even expecting her to?* I thought back about the same girl who had opened her window only half way down to talk to me. Today, she had thrown back my pen and dashed off thanklessly. I blamed myself for the agitation I felt. I shouldn't have given her my notes; I shouldn't have spoken to her that morning; I shouldn't have told the whole story of Ammi's heart attack. I didn't know her and, to be fair, I didn't even want to.

I walked up the stairs to check if Dr Saleh was in. To my good fortune, his door was half open. He was on the phone explaining to someone a flaw in Plato's Eutopia. I didn't want to knock and disturb. I stood there for about fifteen minutes waiting for him to come off the phone. As soon as he said goodbye and I heard the receiver hit the cradle, I knocked at the door.

"Come in, come in! Salik! Where've you been?"

"Sir, Sorry, I was away. I had to go to Faisalabad in an emergency …"

"Okay, so what brings you here today?"

"I just wanted to thank you for a good read …"

He had the habit of cutting halfway and speaking in

"Thank you for my thesis?" He had the habit of cutting people off halfway, "Why should you be thankful? I wrote it for the University. They said thanks by awarding me a degree. What makes you so thankful?"

He finished off with his big laughter.

"No ... but yes Sir ... but ... I wanted to thank you for giving me a copy. It's been a real eye-opener. I never knew what our true history was. I never saw Pakistan in this perspective. I realised now that I've been cheated all my life with false stories. We all get cheated by these Mullah driven syllabi ..."

"Quite right. It is a tragedy. We've robbed one generation after the other of the true face of history. We try and blame foreign powers for everything that goes wrong in Pakistan, not knowing that we, ourselves, are responsible for the malignant evils that lurk in every nook and cranny of our society. Take a look at the history of Islam. It's been self-sufficient regarding harm. Muslims have never left room for any external force to come and destroy them. They made their own heroes and then decided to kill them. Who killed The Four Great Imams of *Fiqh?* Muslims! Who killed Tariq bin Ziad? Muslims! And if you want to come down to modern times? Who killed Shah Faisal al-Saud? His Muslim nephew!

Who hanged Bhutto the Muslim? Another Muslim called Ziaul Haq! Liaqat Ali Khan took credit for turning Pakistan into a theocracy. Who killed him? Yet again, another Muslim. Why so? Because everyone thought that others didn't fit the definition of a Muslim, and hence, deserved to be killed. Why would foreign powers even waste time in trying to kill a self-destructive nation? Muslims are murdering Islam? Why blame others!"

There was no laughter at the end of this long statement. I could see sorrow and passion come together in Dr Saleh's eyes. He was grief stricken by the situation of Pakistan where the state religion was Islam but where no one was ready to accept the other as Muslim. I couldn't agree more.

The laughter that Dr Saleh punctuated every sentence with was perhaps a shield. To hide the sorrow he had in his heart for his country; the country that lay on its deathbed, waiting for the plug to be pulled. He had to hide behind his laughter so no one could see the grief in his eyes; the grief that hits you when bereavement of a loved one is just round the corner, and you happen to know.

CHAPTER ELEVEN

As I walked back to my hostel, I recalled the meeting with Akhtar that morning. His story had left me perplexed, but lectures, assignments and my meeting with Dr Saleh had put that puzzle on halt. Now that I walked back to my room, the confusion had come back to life. I was going to see Akhtar again who lived a secret life. It was a different Akhtar that I was going to see. I had known him all along as a decent chap from a small town called Chiniot located on the banks of the great River Chenab. The river that crossed the whole of the Pakistani Punjab. It started to flow from the foot of the Great Himalayas, covered a small patch of Kashmir before entering the plains of the Punjab, flowed through most part of the Punjab plains and crossed the border of Sind before falling into the Mighty Indus near Rajanpur.

The only time I had heard of Chiniot before knowing Akhtar was when Abbaji had bought some solid wooden four-poster bed for Dado and had boastfully told that it was made in Chiniot. So Chiniot, before knowing Akhtar, was nothing but a huge timber yard and furniture factory in my mind, though I'd never thought much about it.

But now Akhtar had revealed, very secretively, that he wasn't actually from Chiniot. He had told me that morning that he did come from the bank of River Chenab but the opposite one, only a few miles from Chiniot. He had been reluctant in saying the name of the town and would give short, silly answers to my questions that made me even more curious.

"So you're not from Chiniot?"

"Not really, but it's not too far away."

"So where are you from then?"

"Erm... You can say I am from Chiniot because it falls in the Chiniot *Tehsil* ..."

"But it's not Chiniot?"

"Well... Yes... I mean no, it isn't Chiniot per se!"

"So where on earth are you from then?"

"The opposite bank of the river!"

I could see that he was avoiding a direct answer to my questions. The more secretive he became, the more curious I got. I was now getting a bit frustrated. He had taken me in confidence; he said that he trusted me because he had seen that I wasn't religious; he knew that I wasn't a hardliner Muslim. Then why was he being so difficult now?

"So the place doesn't have a name! You live in a tent by the river?" I was now on the brink of losing my temper.

"Well, it has a name. You promise that this will end here and you won't ever mention this to anyone, right?"

"Yes, I promise! I swear I won't mention it! Why would I? Now go on and tell me if you want, if you don't let's just go back. It's not like I'm dying to know!"

"I'm from Rabwah. A small town by the River Chenab."

"Ok," I said, in anticipation for more detail.

He looked at me in astonishment as if expecting me to react differently. "So this doesn't change your opinion about me?"

"Of course it doesn't! Why would it make a difference to me if someone's from Lahore or Karachi or Multan or this town of yours or wherever?"

He then went into the details of why he had been so reluctant to tell me. The detail of why he had introduced himself as being from Chiniot when he actually wasn't. The detail didn't make any sense to me. He said that he belonged to a certain Muslim sect called Ahmadi.

"Ahmadi ... Never heard of that," I had openly shown my ignorance. "Why does that make you so vulnerable that you have to hide your affiliation? Everyone around here is from one sect or another, so what's different about your sect?"

"There's actually something else. I'm just surprised you've never heard about us!"

"Akhtar, I haven't believed in religion for a very long time. I haven't been bothered about sectarianism and the rubbish that comes in the package. Maybe that's why!"

"You seem to care so much about the Pakistani society and the way it's breaking down to tatters. Religion has a great role to play in all of this. If you don't get to know the role of religion in our society, you can't ever get to the root cause," he now sounded more certain than ever. More confident than I had ever seen him.

"Akhtar! I think you just want to feel special."

I tried to joke, but Akhtar's response left my joke out of place.

"But I think you're unaware of a problem that is a bedrock of all our problems. I'm surprised you've been studying political science for the past six months at master's level, and you haven't even discovered where the problem of our society actually lies."

As we got back from the cafeteria and walked into the hallway of the hostel, he said that we would talk about it later.

Soon I was back in the hallway of the hostel. Before going to my room, I thought I should head straight to the mess and have lunch. The mess was bustling with hungry, young men trying to pacify at least one basic instinct while the other was under the strict supervision of *Jamiat.* The chit chat on the tables would make the mess quite noisy at such times. Everyone wanted to get to the mess at the earliest moment of serving times to get the best out of the steaming pots as they got pulled off the massive burners of the kitchen. *Chapatis* were also at their best before they were wrapped up in hot-pots for late-comers.

I was devouring the potatoes and leftover pieces of meat sinking at the bottom of the soup with soggy *chapati* when I saw Akhtar walking out of the mess.

"Akhtar!" I called out loud.

I asked him if he wanted to go out for a stroll by the canal and, in minutes, we were walking by one of the most beautiful walkways of Lahore. It was mid-afternoon of a Pakistani midsummer, so the temperatures were soaring high. Our room was on the top floor of the hostel, so it was always roasting during noons and afternoons, leaving someone like me no choice but to find a cooler place in the campus. The walkway by the canal was the best spot one could find. There was peace, there was tranquillity, natural beauty, plenty of shade, and there was the fresh flowing water of the canal that ran like an artery through the city of Lahore, crossed the campus of Punjab University and flowed on to fall in the BRB Canal near the borders with India.

I didn't want to sound intimidating and inquisitive, so I decided not to touch the topic of his sect and his town where he had lived all his life and naturally loved it very fondly.

Akhtar turned the tables and, as we walked past the willow trees along the canal, asked me why I didn't believe in religion. I tried to cut a long story short.

"I just can't believe in some scary being sitting in the heavens, waiting to punish me for everything I did. And the concept of this being in the heavens pleasing himself by seeing people praise him and bow to him is just beyond my understanding. I can't believe in him, not to speak of loving him as he expects."

"Who said he's in the heavens?"

"Everyone! My parents, your parents, the so-called prophets, the Quran, the Maulvis. They all say so! They even look up and stare at the skies when praying to him. It's all so unscientific."

"You dragged my parents in, but they never said so," Akhtar remained unmoved with my blasphemous comments about his God. I didn't expect him to remain so calm because he had told me that morning that he was not only a believer but a staunch believer and prayed five times a day to this God of his.

"Well... Wherever he is, I'm just sick and tired of the whole concept. He wants us to bow to him so he can be happy; he himself created a Satan to lead us astray so he can be unhappy with us; then he wants us to beg so he can forgive; he inflicts hardships so we can call him for help. And then he chooses whether to come for help or not! I'm sorry, I don't get this 'omnipotent' god of yours."

I looked at his face as I said this, maybe because I thought that he should react now. But he didn't. I don't know why, but I wanted him to. I decided to push a bit more.

"Now I ask you the same question you asked me this morning."

"What?"

"All this doesn't change your opinion about me, does it?"

The Akhtar that was in a panic last night and even this morning was absolutely calm. "No! It doesn't"

"Thank you very much!" I continued to push harder. I had a punch-bag where I could take it all out, but Akhtar continued trying to sell me 'his' god.

"You see, what you're doing is what God Himself asks us to do. In the Quran, there are hundreds of occasions where He says 'why don't you think?', 'why don't you ponder?', 'why, then don't you use reason'. The whole Quran is full of such commandments where God wants us to reflect and use our minds to understand Him, so you've ended up actually obeying the God you don't believe in".

Akhtar left me dumbfounded. He was using my *disbelief* to prove that I actually *believed* in god. I got defensive.

"Okay, I don't remember reading any such verse in the many times that I read the Quran. Maybe you guys believe in some other Quran, and that is why your sect has asked for trouble."

"No! It's exactly the same Quran we believe in. Did you ever read the translation?"

"No, but …" I wanted to argue on

"Well, there you go. Do you know Arabic?"

"No, but …" I tried again, but he wouldn't let me say a word.

"Then how could you understand the meaning. I think you should have understood the Quran before you dismissed it."

"My mother made me memorise certain verses. Then Maulvi Sahib had regular classes where he would tell us the gist of most of the Quran."

"Salik, I don't expect this from an educated, modern person like you. You never felt like understanding its meaning, and you declared it redundant. That makes you more of a Maulvi than a liberal."

Akhtar had cornered me, but I still didn't want to give up,

"Anyway, the god I have been introduced to is just not worth believing in!"

"No one can introduce you to God. You have to find your God for yourself. It takes a lot of effort to get to know your God. I can introduce you to mine, a Maulvi can introduce you to his, a mother can introduce you to hers, but a God you believe in has to be *your* God. Your very own God."

We had come quite far in both distance and discussion.

"Shall we turn back?" I asked.

"You turn back, Salik," replied the evangelist in Akhtar.

"I mean shall we make our way back now?" I laughed. Luckily, Akhtar got the joke. I hadn't seen him laugh since the previous night. We all need to get things off our chest from time to time.

I left the disputed god on the outskirts of the campus as we walked back. Akhtar must have brought his back with him. We talked and laughed about various aspects of the university, our childhoods, our families, our college life and what not.

By the time we got back to the hostel, the sun had dropped towards the horizon, where it would finally set. The trees by the canal were casting shadows longer than their own tall bodies. We stopped at Rafiq's stall for tea. As soon as Rafiq slammed his saucepan on the gas-burner, the air became laden with the breath-taking aroma of tea that floated around with the wind.

CHAPTER TWELVE

E xams approached sooner than I had expected. I had always been good at studying for exams as I rarely got distracted by things going on around me. But the thought of Ammi being ill would come back to my mind even though I would try to brush it away. I decided to make use of the upcoming weekend and travel to Faisalabad. As I waited at the campus gates for a rickshaw, I hoped to find the same driver who had taken me to the coach station the other day. But not all hopes materialise in life. I sat in the first rickshaw that stood at the front of the broken and dotted queue of rickshaws, and I was soon on my way. This driver turned out to be relatively quieter. He seemed so preoccupied with his own problems that he wouldn't bother to listen to others'. Maybe he didn't have a wife whose prayers always got answered.

"How much?" I asked as I got off at the coach station.

"A hundred!" he replied briefly.

I handed him a hundred rupees out of the two hundred that I had borrowed from my roommate, Salim. Living in Lahore wasn't as easy as it was to live in Faisalabad. Abbaji would give me two thousand rupees every month which was hardly enough to pay off the mess dues and hostel fees. What was left was only sufficient to pay the *dhobi* at the campus laundrette. Travelling to and from Faisalabad was a luxury that I could not afford. I had no plans of taking up this luxury very often, but Ammi's illness would not let me sit in peace. I had to see her. Some triggers are hard to avoid.

That morning, my eyes had caught Shamaila's earrings but, unfortunately, at a moment when a lock of her hair had got caught in them. She was struggling, very carefully, to release them from the trap. This had been reminiscent of Ammi doing the same when I would play with her *jhumka,* and a lock of her hair would sometimes get trapped. This alone was enough to make me want to visit home. The trigger was so strong that I ended up borrowing money from Salim not knowing how I would pay it off; there was no sign of the cycle of my pocket-money changing. Hostel fees, mess dues and the laundry were all going to have their fair share and leave me with little money but not as much as to repay the debt. But I had to see Ammi. So, I thought that I would request Abbaji for an increment in my monthly allowance. I was very hopeful to get a positive response.

The coach driver took half an hour less than it usually would take to get to Faisalabad from Lahore. *Hashish can do wonders,* I thought and smiled as I caught sight of the driver's bloodshot eyes in his rear-view mirror.

The night was setting in as I got off at the coach station. The typical stench welcomed me back; urine, rotting fruit, banana skin, roasted peanuts and diesel fumes; the amalgamation that creates the peculiar smell that travels in the air of all coach stations in Pakistan.

I thought I would give them a surprise, but I was surprised by what awaited me.

Firstly, Abbaji replied to my *Salam* which he had to for religious reasons, but then opened a rapid round of questions.

"How come you're back?" "How did you get the ticket; how much was it?" "I thought you said your exams were getting closer. How did you spare this time to travel? I don't want to see you fail or else I want you back sitting in the shop helping me. I'm already struggling to make ends meet."

Ammi was as robotic as ever. She greeted me, kissed my forehead, looked keenly at my face as if to make sure that I really was alright as I had said, and then she disappeared into the kitchen where I could hear her rolling pin, rolling out chapatis on the wooden worktop. She didn't feel the need to ask if I was going to have dinner. Mothers don't need to ask if we are hungry, they just know it.

Abbaji seemed distressed. Aunties and Uncles all went away to their rooms sooner than they normally would. There seemed to be some kind of tension.

Abbaji was lying in the veranda listening to the news on the radio. The big pedestal fan was roaring nearby. I grabbed a stool and sat in the farthest corner of the semi-circular range of the revolving pedestal fan. I wanted to avoid further questioning but wanted a bit of air. But Abbaji was probably waiting for me to settle down.

"It's all over. The love, the unity, the mutual support of us brothers. It only lasts until parents live. I knew they were waiting for your Dado to die. They both want their share. They say they've had enough of this seed business. They think they will invest in some other business and become millionaires overnight. I'm giving them their share and leaving them to do what they want."

Abbaji sounded deeply distressed and depressed.

"And what will you do?" I had hardly ever asked a straight forward question to Abbaji in my life.

"Me? Well! ..."

I could tell he wasn't clear. I had never seen him think before he spoke all my life, so his mind must have been really clouded. He must be too unsure about the future, but he continued.

"... I'll carry on. I'm having to downsize the business though. I've found a smaller shop from where I can keep it going. I'll have to rely more on taking orders on the phone and delivering them. I might just use the new shop as storage. I didn't expect I'd have to go through this bullshit at this age. Anyway, how long before you get your degree?"

I knew this was coming. It had only been a few weeks when I told him it was going to be another year and a half. But the almighty Abbaji was asking, so I had to reiterate,

"Another eighteen months."

I did feel very strongly for Abbaji, but I didn't want to wage war by declaring that I wasn't going into the seed business after my degree.

The food had the same delicious taste, but the atmosphere in the *haweli* seemed to have turned it sour. The *chapatis* had the same aroma of ground, cooked wheat and the feel of the farmlands of Punjab where it was grown. They still had the warmth of the sun that had ripened the wheat before it was thrashed by farmers, sweating in the scorching heat of Punjabi summers. What was missing in those *chappatis* that night was the peace of mind they had always brought with them. Our moods can creep in and settle into what we cook.

Abbaji was too huge a figure for me to console. Although I wanted to, I simply couldn't muster up the courage to sympathise. And the consolation he actually wanted from me, was the one I didn't want to offer. I had a career before me that I was going to pursue, rather than run a shop in the Aminpur Bazaar of Faisalabad. But I couldn't just walk away. "I hope it all goes well!" That was all I could say before getting up to go into Ammi's room.

Her health looked better. Even if she wasn't feeling fine, she would never have said so, but I could see that she didn't seem as weak and frail as I had left her a few weeks ago. As I talked to her, I placed my head on Ammi's shoulder. I had done so after many, many years. I felt complete serenity. *But I'm a fully grown man! What am I doing?* I took my head off her shoulder and sat up straight. I thought why I had done so; I wasn't used to expressing love. Was it because I had missed her, or was it because I wanted to see her *jhumkay* up close; the jhumkay I had always played with when I was young. The *jhumkay* that had now become a character in the drama of my life. I wanted to get a feel of them just once again. I thought she wouldn't notice, but as soon as I touched one of the *jhumkas*, she asked, "How is your Shamaila?"

"*My* Shamaila?! I told you there's nothing like that. She's just a girl like any other one in my class. It's just that she wears the same *jhumkay* as yours. That's it!"

She only smiled as she got up to put the dry laundry back in the closets. As she folded Abbaji's clothes, I could see on her face the solemn loyalty she had for her husband. As if she was in worship! Her son, who now lived far away in Lahore and whom she hardly ever got to see now, was sitting before her but the touch of her husband's clothes sent her in a trance. *What a life!* I thought how caught up she was in an in-between feeling of love and fear. I took leave to go to bed.

"Pray for your Father. He's worried. The *haweli* has broken apart. Your uncles no longer want this joint business. Don't know what's gone wrong. Maybe it's someone's curse that's shattered the love and peace of our family," she said as she neatly folded away Abbaji's clothes.

Life for most of us in our society is all about prayer and curse. This is what holds back our society from progress. This is why we don't want to work hard in life. We sit and wait for our prayers to be accepted, and when nothing happens, we think it's a curse that isn't giving way to prosperity.

I fell asleep with these 'blasphemous' thoughts. The next thing I remember is Abbaji waking me up,

"It's time for Prayer! Get up quick! I'm going to the mosque."

I had to wake up, I had to go to the mosque, and I had to act the *Namaz* to please Abbaji's god. During the *namaz*, I thought about the two hundred rupees I had to return to Salim. Where would they come from? The hope of getting an increment from Abbaji had flown out of the window with the story of the crisis that he was going through. I didn't pray in *namaz* as I didn't believe in it and also because all that time, I was too busy working out how I was going to pay back the debt. I didn't believe that prayers could arrange the money I needed.

I had always loved the early mornings of the *haweli*. We would walk home from the mosque when it was hardly daybreak. The *haweli* was all awake, and life was set to take off for the day. But that morning, the *haweli* wasn't buzzing with life. It was dull and sombre. Uncle Ashraf was brushing his teeth at the washbasin in the courtyard. Everyone was awake but had decided to stay in their own rooms.

"*Salam*," I said as Uncle put his toothbrush away on one of the protruding bricks of the wall.

"*Salam*," he replied, with a smile that wasn't very natural. He tapped my shoulder and went back to his room from where I could hear Aunty Amna reciting the Quran loud enough to make it echo in the *haweli*. It was believed that reciting the Quran aloud in the early hours of the day brought good fortune to the household. All my family members had done so all these decades. I wondered where the good fortune was. All I saw was a family stricken by nothing but misfortune.

Ammi was already making *Paratha*s in the kitchen. I walked in,

"Remind me, why are we having breakfast so early?"

"We always have it early, don't we?"

"Yeah, but I wanted to catch up on my sleep. Or do you just want me to eat and rush back to Lahore?"

"If it was up to me, I wouldn't ever want you to go back. It's just that your Aunties have to cook their breakfast. We no longer cook together. Everyone cooks for their own family."

This was the first time I'd seen the sorrow of this breakup on Ammi's face. The kitchen having fallen apart is what meant more than anything else to her. The kitchen is undoubtedly the capital of a woman's territory. It had been taken by the forces of misfortune.

She put a *paratha* on the pan and looked out of the window as if to make sure no one was around. Whispering in my ear, she began to untie a knot on her shawl. This had always been her bank.

"I saved this for you. Get something nice for yourself. Or eat something of your choice."

She secretly slipped the rolled up stack of twenty-rupee-notes from her hand into mine. I knew she didn't want me to argue or else Abbaji would know this secret. Money matters would fly first to Abbaji's eardrums before anywhere else, so I didn't say a word. I hugged her. I had hugged her after a very long time. But I felt a difference that touched my heart. Her body felt weak and frail. I was now taller than her, so I also got to see that most of her hair had turned grey. The parting in her hair had grown wider. From up there, I got to see her hands on the rolling pin. Her skin was ageing, and wrinkles were gradually beginning to form all around. *Some realities are harsh*, I thought as I just walked out of the kitchen.

I wanted to just get out of the *haweli* quickly. So as soon as I had finished my breakfast, I got ready to leave.

CHAPTER THIRTEEN

When I arrived at the hostel, it was already dusk. It had only started to get dark. Everyone seemed to be rushing towards the mosque. I thought about the village mosque where I had enacted the prayer ritual that morning. I knew that most of them would be imagining all sorts of silly things while performing the sit-stand-bow ritual just as I had thought of Salim's debt during the whole course of *namaz*.

Oh no! That reminded me of the loan. I was going to see Salim again, and he would expect it to be paid back. *Gosh!*

Shall I pay it off from the monthly allowance that Abbaji had given me for the following month? But what will I do of the hostel fees and mess dues? Or shall I just wait for him to ask? But that won't seem right and would breach trust. So what do I do? I was out of solutions. Our minds can either cripple in panic or work faster. I was lucky that mine worked faster on that occasion. I thought I would try and find a part-time job and then pay off his debt soon. A promise of few weeks' time shouldn't sound too bad. I had reached a decision before even reaching my room. I walked into my room to find both my roommates there

"*Salam.*"

"*Salam,*" they both replied.

Akhtar was unpacking his bag.

"Where have you been Akhtar?" I asked.

"I had to go home to get money for some books. Just got back!"

"From Chiniot?" I said in a tongue-in-cheek tone.

He turned around to see what Salim was doing. Assured that Salim hadn't taken notice, he replied with a smile.

"Yeah, where else?" he said, showing his clenched fist.

All three of us had a good chat before it was decided to have dinner at Rafiq's stall. Salim said he had to go for prayer in the mosque and suggested we have dinner after that.

"Hey, you bloody infidels, why don't you guys say *Namaz?*"

All three of us laughed as he walked out of the room with a white cotton cap on his head.

Akhtar said he also had to go somewhere and would be back before Salim. Saying this, he went to his cupboard, took something out and put it in his pocket. He thought I wouldn't, but I had noticed,

"What's that?" I asked.

"What?"

"That thing you just shoved in your pocket!"

"Oh, this?" He took out the white cotton cap, just like Salim's

"Are you going for *Namaz*?"

"Erm... yes."

"I thought you were too scared of belonging to that sect of yours."

"I'll tell you later." A quick reply and he was gone.

I thought I should freshen up in the meantime. I took off my wristwatch and my red-stone-in-silver ring and was emptying my pockets when my hand hit the stack of folded up notes that Ammi had given me in the morning.

I took them and folded them straight so I could count the money that my dear mother had so fondly saved up for me. Twenty, forty, sixty ... The notes, some with stains of *paan*, others with small bits of dried up dough, amounted to three hundred. I took a sigh of relief. Two hundred to pay off Salim's debt and the rest to have Rafiq's *Dal Chawal* about ten times if I only paid for myself. But only paying for yourself is not taken to be a decent act in the society of Pakistan that thrives on clichés. But then you have others who pay for you when it's their turn. So although it turns out to be the same as paying for yourself at the end, but customs seem to take the best side of us when it comes to culture.

I sorted the notes by putting the ones with small, dried up bits of dough aside and counted two hundred from the remaining to give back to Salim as soon as he got back. I knew that Akhtar always came back earlier than Salim after the prayer-breaks, so I thought I wouldn't pay Salim in Akhtar's presence. I didn't want it to be publicly known that I was struggling with my expenses; loans only come in when we spend beyond our means.

I put the money along with the allowance in the lockable drawer within my closet, keeping thirty rupees out to spend at Rafiq's, in case my offer to pay for all three of us got accepted. I made sure I wasn't taking the five notes that had Ammi's signature on them; the tiny bits of dried up dough. I could imagine Ammi tying them to her shawl as she cooked in the kitchen because that is the only privacy our women have. Our men hardly ever decide to step in the kitchen to help.

As soon as Salim and Akhtar got back from pleasing their gods, we walked down to the food stalls. All of Rafiq's tables were taken, and once a table was taken, it could stay occupied until late night because students would sit in groups and chat forever. And Rafiq, nice and kind as he was, wouldn't ask anyone to leave even if they had given him very little business. He was too busy shouting at his waiters to take the orders to the tables. As we stood there waiting for a table, Rafiq's eye caught us waiting.

"Come on over here, you can sit at the back!" he shouted loud enough to be heard. We felt privileged as we walked towards the exclusive table that he had got laid for us at the back of the stall where pots and cutlery were being washed up. It wasn't ideal, but it was great. We ate and talked about all sorts of things. Salim was very open in talking about his childhood, his family, the colony in Gujrat that he lived in, his father's job, his brother's business and everything to do with him. I too was quite open about myself. But Akhtar would only give a vague outline of events when it was his turn to add his share, that too when it was inevitable. This careful editing of detail had become his second nature, and it was very obvious that he didn't have to put in a lot of effort to edit out any details that could lead his audience to cross the bridge on River Chenab and get to the other side.

It was almost midnight when we got out of Rafiq's stall and went to our room. It was the first time we had sat together for so long. This long sitting made us even better friends. What created the bond more than anything was that all three of us were quite like minded. We talked less about people and more about ideas. All credit went to Akhtar because he would lead the discussions and keep them restricted to ideas and not anything else. Maybe because he was a student of Philosophy. Or maybe because he didn't want the conversation to derail and head into areas where he had to show his personal side. The more we speak, the higher the chances of truth floating to surface.

The next morning, I paid back the loan to Salim after Akhtar had left for his department. I felt a deep sense of love and gratitude for my mother. God knew I was in need but didn't come to help; Ammi didn't know, but she came to help. She was more divine than god. Had I told Akhtar about all this, he would have credited god for the arrangement.

I didn't feel as relieved as one would after paying back a loan. I was stuck with how I was going to manage my expenses in future. There was no chance of an increment from Abbaji in my monthly allowance. Rather, I wanted to stop asking for money because I knew that I was his biggest expense-head. I had to find a part-time job, and by the time I walked off the canal bank towards the grand corridor, I had decided that the search would have to start immediately after classes. How? I didn't know.

I saw Dr Saleh walking towards the department from the other end of the corridor. And along him walked Shamaila, giggling, joking, and chatting as usual. I wondered what she might be saying to him. All three of us approached the classroom at the same time.

"Sir, stay away from this guy! He's a crook!"

She laughed as she ran into the classroom.

"What have you done to this girl that she thinks you're a crook? I thought you were a nice guy!" said Dr Saleh, smiling.

"Sir, you know how girls often exaggerate! But how are you, Sir?"

"I'm good, I'm good! And you?"

Before I could reply, Dr Saleh went on.

"By the way, come and see me after classes. I've got something for you."

Humbled by his kind invitation and the thought that a learned scholar like Dr Saleh had got something for me, I walked into the lecture room.

There was only one vacant chair in the whole room; the one behind Shamaila. This daughter of a bureaucrat, who thought she was a queen, had placed the whole pile of her books on that chair.

"Pick these up! Keep them with you!" I whispered as I approached the chair, trying not to interrupt the lecture that had already started.

"Shut Up! Keep standing! You won't die. Or balance them on your head if you want to."

This is who she was. She was just being herself. A carefree, happy, jolly daughter of a bureaucrat who thought that the world revolves around her. I picked the books up and used them as my table to take notes from the lecture. It was sheer agony writing in a notebook that was almost at the same height as my eyes.

There was no lecture afterwards for the next two hours, so as soon as it finished, everyone dispersed in different groups, in different directions. I couldn't get up because I had to wait for Shamaila to rid me of this burden of knowledge resting on my legs.

"You're so lazy, Salik! Couldn't you just put them away on the shelves at the back?"

"Nice! I'm lazy, right! And what does that make you?"

"The lecture had started when I came in. I can't afford to miss a single word, that too when exams are lurking around. I'm not as clever as you are 'professor' Salik! I have to work hard."

She picked up half the books, and I took the rest with her to the shelves at the back of the classroom. I wanted to rush out lest we got seen, the two of us, all by ourselves. I couldn't afford to take the infamous torture of *Jamiat* for being with a girl who I didn't have anything to do with. I turned around and had just walked a few steps when she called out.

"Salik! Dad said he wants a tutor for my sister. She struggles with maths and chemistry. She's doing O Levels. I thought I should ask if you could help."

"Yeah, sure! I'm sure I'll find someone in my hostel. There're many science students around. I'll let you know."

I was only half-turned towards her so I could keep walking as I replied.

"No!"

I had to stop again.

"What now?"

"Can you not teach her in the evenings? I know you only walk around the campus all evening staring at girls. No girl is going to come your way! Do something productive!"

"Maths? And chemistry? You must be joking! It's been ages since I last touched anything to do with these subjects. I've been a humanities guy all along. I'll find someone fit for this and let you know. I've got to go now. I don't want to be seen with you by *Jamiat*. They might think I'm flirting. I'll see you later!"

I was out of the classroom, headed to the canteen. I couldn't wait to see Dr Saleh at the end of classes in the afternoon.

CHAPTER FOURTEEN

"Sir, May I come in?"

"Yes of course! Please, do come in Salik."

Dr Saleh now seemed to be in his usual mood. He was all laughter at the start and end of every sentence.

He started digging in his big bag. His bag was the type of a briefcase-on-wheels that pharmaceutical agents carry around with samples of medicines to promote at surgeries and clinics. He was trying to find what he was looking for, but before he could start the search, he got carried away with emptying his bag of rubbish. Train tickets, book vouchers, receipts all creased and folded away in an unsymmetrical manner, scrunched up sand-wich wrappers and even a cotton-bud. All this was coming out of his magic satchel and ending up in his wastebasket. "This, and this, and that too..." he murmured as he cleared up his bag, chuck-ling and sniggering at every piece of rubbish that emerged.

"Ah! Finally! Here you go, Salik!"

He passed me a huge stack of papers; a whole ream of printed paper.

"Thank you, Sir!" The obedient Pakistani boy in me spoke up every time I talked to a teacher

He laughed. "Well, aren't you going to ask what it is?"

"What is it, Sir?" I asked with utmost respect

"Nothing special. It's the manuscript of my book. I was about to send it to the publishers. But you know how fussy they are."

I looked at him in astonishment as he spoke.

"I thought I should get a few opinions on it be-fore I send it off. Try to be as critical as you can. I'll see you tomorrow!"

He didn't forget to laugh, but even before I had got up from the chair, he had picked up the phone and was already dialling a number. He didn't even give me the chance to ask why he was putting me through this test. How could a student, who had just landed in the university, review his book? What did he actually mean? Would I even be able to comment on such scholarly work?

I was about to walk out when he gestured to remain seated. He was connected on the phone to someone.

"Yes, Saleh speaking."

He chuckled. Then there was a pause while the person on the other end spoke, and Dr Saleh replied in laughter. Again a pause followed by another chuckle. "Okay, I'll call you later."

I couldn't help bursting out in laughter myself. I had to let it out, so I did.

"What happened? Why are you laughing?"

I had to tell him the truth. "Sir, what kind of a conversation was that? You just laughed back at everything!" I asked very frankly.

"It was a good friend of mine. She is in Karachi University. She speaks non-stop and always has a reason to have a go at me. I could only laugh back."

A very friendly side of Dr Saleh emerged that day. Maybe he liked people who burst into laughter like him. He saw me laugh out loud and he took me to be almost a friend of his.

"What are you doing right now?"

"Nothing special, Sir."

"Have you had lunch?"

"No, Sir"

"Ok Sir, Let's go, Sir, Let's have Lunch Sir, Shall we Sir? What's wrong with you man? Why do you keep calling me 'Sir'? Take it easy boy. Let's have something nice to eat."

We continued to talk as he locked the door behind him. His car was parked quite close to the department. I never knew that lecturers had reserved parking bays in the campus.

"I thought there was no respect for teachers in Pakistan, but it's good to see that you have an allocated parking bay."

"No, there's a lot of respect for you in Pakistan if you have a car. You don't have to be a teacher for that," he laughed again. This impressed me. He was a very thoughtful man. Even his jokes stemmed out of the deep understanding of the society. He had understood our society in so much depth that he couldn't help but laugh at it; he would laugh at you, at anyone and even at his own self. Tragedy alone gives you the courage to laugh at your own self, and he had the guts.

"What do you like in food?" he asked as soon he drove from the car park onto the Canal Bank Road towards Muslim Town.

"Anything," I said but couldn't help adding the suffix "Sir!"

"Chinese?" He asked. He knew I wouldn't give consent, so he imposed it on me.

We drove down along the canal before turning on to Ferozepur Road, leaving it at Main Boulevard and then pulling into a bay outside a Chinese restaurant in Liberty Market.

The aura of the restaurant was very impressive. It was the first time in my life that I was seated in a Chinese restaurant. I was impressed but didn't want it to be too obvious. "I'll have whatever you're having, Sir," I said this quickly to avoid the embarrassment of not knowing even a single dish on the menu card.

As we waited for food, Dr Saleh threw question after question at me. I had a feeling that he wanted to know about me just as much as I wanted to know him.

"So we have a young man from Faisalabad whose father sells seeds in Aminpur Bazar, and he says he enjoyed reading my thesis. This is rather strange, isn't it? No one takes out the time to read that big stack, and you say you read it in one night. If I asked you to tell me what struck you the most, what would you say?"

"Sir, I felt that you've read the pulse of our society very well. You brought it all down to religion. I never knew that all those who considered Islam their saviour were using nothing but Islam itself for their own destruction."

I was surprised to see that he was listening attentively.

"Hmm. So you agree?"

"I agree, Sir, but not everyone seems to do so."

"Not everyone can anyway. If everyone agreed with this, you wouldn't be doing a master's degree in political science. And I wouldn't be getting paid to teach you. You would be selling seeds like your father, and I would be driving a rickshaw or whipping the backside of a donkey."

I now felt comfortable laughing aloud at his jokes. He knew how to keep discussions lively.

The food was really good but even better was the discussion we had. We spoke about the political climate in Pakistan and how it was intertwined with religion. How the combination had turned malignant and how it was decaying the society from within. We spoke about *Jamiat* and its origins and its forefathers. He told me how *Jamiat* had originated in the name of religion but turned out to be a terror group.

As he talked about how some Islamic sects had terrorised other Islamic sects, and the gravity of the persecution that some had to go through, I got flashbacks of the panic attacks that Akhtar had had the other day. I interrupted.

"Sir, there is one thing though. It surprises me to see that you've made no mention of Ahmadis in your thesis. I've just very recently come to know that they too are severely discriminated against."

"No, who says I missed them out. About half of chapter five is all about them! So you haven't read it carefully. Now I know how you managed to read it overnight."

"No Sir, I read it entirely and with great care."

"Then how could you miss it? I wrote about ten thousand words about Quadianis."

"Quadianis? No, I'm talking about Ahmadis."

"It's one and the same thing. They call themselves Ahmadis, but our society knows them as Quadiani. So I used this term to refer to them."

"So you did. I'm sorry I didn't know this. But... Erm... Okay."

"What is it?" he asked, "Just say it..."

Dr Saleh studied my facial expressions and noticed that I wasn't coming to the point.

"What makes you so curious about this sect? Don't tell me you're a Quadiani, are you?"

"Oh no Sir, I'm not. I'm just thinking that ... Forget it! It's best I read the chapter again, and we can carry on with this."

"Anytime! Feel free. Just make sure you aren't too loud in mentioning them. Or you too shall be branded a Quadiani. Anyone showing sympathy with them is taken to be a Quadiani, which means an agent for the Jews, the British, the Indians or all three. So be careful!"

The discussion went on even after we had eaten. From Quadianis, or Ahmadis, from Shiites to the

Ismailis. From religion to education and from education to sociology and anthropology.

A new Dr Saleh had dawned upon me. He was a fountainhead of knowledge. You could talk to him about anything, and he would speak on the topic forever.

He dropped me back at the campus entrance from where I took my favourite walkway and walked down towards my hostel.

So that means Akhtar's a Quadiani! Could he really be an agent? Does he still think I would harm him? All I thought about during the short walk was Akhtar and his strange faith.

I could recall coming across the term Quadiani on many occasions. The Maulvi Sahib at the mosque would often tell us about them and would emphasise that we stayed away from them. They were blasphemous to the Prophet. They had a prophet of their own. They said their prophet was actually God personified. They had to swear at the Prophet to remain a Quadiani. Abbaji had once told me to stay away from a boy at school who was from a Quadiani family. Then one day, a Quadiani family had sent us sweets at the birth of a son and Dado had asked Ammi to throw it away, not even in the bin, but somewhere outside far away from the *haweli*. I recalled carrying it in a plastic shopping bag, holding it like a soiled nappy, making sure it didn't touch my body. That's how I was told to handle the 'accursed' bag.

The Muslim in me awoke as I thought about Quadianis. The hate instilled in one's mind in childhood rarely ever goes away. But I didn't believe in Islam and in the Prophet who started it all. Religion, in my view, spread nothing but hatred. I had given up religion for such reasons anyway, so I managed to not shake my opinion about Akhtar. I took the staircase to my room feeling enlightened by having been in the company of a great scholar and that too in such a refreshing atmosphere. There were so many sides to him, and today I had seen his very scholarly, yet a friendly, side.

CHAPTER FIFTEEN

"So when are you starting? Today or tomorrow? Or are you ever going to start?"

Shamaila always had something to take me by surprise.

"Start what?"

"To teach my sister. You're not a professor, so stop pretending that you've got too much on your plate."

I sighed heavily, "I forgot to ask Salim. He should be able to help. He's studied sciences."

"I'm not having strangers in my house! So WHEN ARE YOU STARTING?"

"Listen Shamaila! First of all, I don't think you'd want me to teach maths and chemistry; I'm not that good at it. Secondly, I don't want to be chased by *Jamiat* for being seen with you. Not that I'm afraid or anything, it's just I can't afford to waste time with all their bullshit."

"One, you're coming to teach her from today. Secondly, as long as Jalal Ali is my father and I'm his daughter, no *Jamiat* is ever going to approach you. So what time? five o'clock? six?"

"You can't take a hint, can you? And by the way, I am taking up a part time job soon, so I wouldn't even have time for this in the afternoons. I'm sorry, but I don't think I can help!"

I tried to sound as firm as I could.

"What job? You wouldn't even be able to spare that many hours after lessons. You only need to spare an hour and a half for this tuition. So tell me, how much will you charge? two thousand?"

She said the exact amount I required to alleviate the burden off my father's frail shoulders. As I thought this, she made another bid,

"Two and a half?"

I was surprised with how the bid had gone up so quickly. Maybe my expression had confused her. But then again, I was more confused.

"Three thousand?"

"Alright! Enough! Three thousand is a lot for only an hour and a half. What are you up to?"

"Done! Three thousand rupees a month. You'll come to our place five days a week with weekends off..."

"But ..."

"But what? No ifs and buts. You're coming over today at six. See you tonight!"

With that, she ran off shouting and screaming at her friends.

That afternoon, as I walked back from the department to my room, I was thinking of what to do now. She had imposed the tuition on me but, to be fair, there wasn't anything wrong with it; I was going to hunt for a job anyway. A job had come my way without even having to search for one, and that too with a salary which I would never have got from a part-time job.

Flipping hell! I froze in my steps. *I don't even know where she lives.* She had tried to guide me the other day, but all I could remember of those vague instructions was to get off the Canal Bank Road at the signpost of Bahria Colony... *but then what?*

I didn't know what to do. I ran back to see if she was still there, but she was gone. One didn't have to ask whether she was around or not. Her presence could be felt if she was. Just to be sure, I checked in classrooms and in the library upstairs. She had definitely left.

I went to the clerk's office to ask if Ghulam Rasool could do anything to help. He was talking to two men seated on the waiting chairs in his office, both dressed in white *shalwar-kamiz*, sandals and beards. They seemed to be having just an informal chit chat, so I jumped in and asked Ghulam Rasool if he could help.

"How would I know? It takes half a set of tea to open up the file and dig out a phone number. Add two samosas if it's a girl's number."

This was typical of Ghulam Rasool. He would make these demands in such a witty way that you wouldn't feel like calling it a bribe.

"Ok, Ghulam Rasool. You'll have that tomorrow. Now can I have her number?"

Ghulam Rasool tiptoed to reach a file with a label that read 'MA Part 1. 1998.'

Moistening the tip of his finger with his tongue, he flicked through the pages. "N ... P ... R ... here we go. S!"

His finger and his eyes that sat behind thick lenses of his glasses ran down the page

"Shamaila Ali... have you got a pen?"

I got the number and was about to leave the room when one of the men sitting on the chairs called me back, pretending to know me,

"*Salam,* Salik *bhai!*"

"*Salam,*" I replied, surprised that he knew me by name.

"Can you come with us please?"

He sounded polite.

"Where to?"

"Hostel 12. Just for a quick word. Won't be too long."

I knew this was *Jamiat*. I didn't know how to react, so I didn't. The two men started to walk ahead of me as I followed them. They would stop after a few steps to talk to students who were dressed like them and had beards. They seemed to be collecting intel of some sort from the guys that bumped into them every minute or so. They appeared to be very respectful in their circle. I picked this from the way they were greeted and how those talking to them would show humility.

I felt awkward as I walked behind them. I had only walked behind Abbaji when we would walk to and from the mosque, but that was many years ago when I was very young.

We walked off the Canal Bank Road walkway towards hostel number twelve. This was the last one in the row of men's hostels. The row of women's hostels started right after this last one, separated by a wall which one could tell wasn't part of the main map of the campus and had been built afterwards.

We walked up the four flights of stairs to get to the second floor of the hostel. I had never been there. It seemed to be occupied by only *Jamiat* because everyone there was dressed in *Jamiat*'s undeclared uniform; *shalwar-kamiz*, a *topi* and a beard.

Every room had its number written on its door. But the door we stood before had no number. The noise of someone swearing could be heard from inside the room.

The door opened, and we walked into the dimly lit room. I was surprised to see an abnormally sized dormitory. Walls had been taken down to turn four rooms into one big hall. The lightbulbs hung from the ceiling, equidistant from each other as they would have when the rooms were in their original form. All walls had banners that read,

Long Live Jamiat, There is no god but Allah, Allaho Akbar. On one of the walls was a poster-size portrait of Maududi, the founder of *Jamiat*. I later learned that he was the one who provided an ideology to Islamist groups that later turned into, what we know today, as terrorist movements.

In the farthest corner was a table where a student sat facing a *Jamiat* goon. I could see that they had paused hurling abuse at him, not knowing if they were expected to carry on. One of the guys that had escorted me gave him a signal to continue, and the Maulvi started to swear and shout at him again.

"If this happens again, I'm going to tie you to two cars and …"

The rest can be imagined. What was funny though was that the guy being sworn at was wearing western clothes and the one using obscene language was dressed in *shalwar-kamiz*, had a beard and was wearing a *topi* on his head; the full 'Islamic' attire. The poor guy was pushed and pulled insultingly out of the room.

I was told to sit on the same chair. Both the *Jamiat* guys that had escorted me to the room pulled their chairs closer. They were still trying to sound polite.

"How are your studies going?" one of them asked.

"They're fine. Could you tell me why I'm here?"

"Just for a quick chat. We're all brothers here. We promote brotherhood and fraternity. We want everyone to live the best way possible: the Islamic way."

I thought I was going to be questioned about the state of my faith.

"Are you related to this girl?"

"Which girl?"

"Whose number you asked for," one of them explained

"And the one you're often seen around with," added the other.

"No. We're not related."

"Then why her number? You see, this is not on. Stop hanging around with her. Let's keep the campus clean and pure. You look like a clever guy. I'm sure you get the hint!"

"Not really, but okay. I've nothing to do with her anyway."

"Look, let's not go down that line. We haven't asked any further questions, so don't push us to ask more. Just remember what you've been told. Be careful."

"Of course." I wanted this to come to an end. Not that I was scared. The atmosphere was just too hostile.

"Thank you. *Salam*."

"*Salam*."

I turned around to see a vagabond holding the door for me. I walked out squinting my eyes as the sunlight seemed brighter as I came out of this gloomy room. It was four o'clock, and I still needed to get Shamaila's address, take a shower, get ready and get to their place.

I had managed to get to the officers' colony and was standing right in front of 23-A, Phase II of Bahria Colony, waiting for the ten minutes to pass before I could ring the bell at six o'clock sharp. I stood there looking at the gigantic bungalows and the palm trees along the avenue that I had walked on to approach the palace-like house. I would look to see whether my watch had struck six, but it too seemed overawed with the splendour of the house and was moving really slow.

There still were a few minutes to six, and I hadn't rung the bell, but I heard a crackle in the intercom by the gate, followed by the question

"Who is it?"

It didn't sound like a family member. The accent was very punjabified, and nothing like one would expect from the inhabitants of such a house. *It must be a servant.*

"Erm… Tutor … to teach … Salik…"

I wasn't ready to be asked who I was so I gave silly answers, all in one go.

I heard the door unlatch.

"Come on in and wait in the veranda."

I walked in and shut the gate behind me. The walk to the veranda was not a very short one. The paved walkway swerved through the lush and neatly cut grass that made up most of the landscape. Two gardeners were busy in different corners of the lawn looking after the garden. I stood on the veranda waiting to be summoned. I looked at the beautiful lawn and the two gardeners working hard to keep the garden in shape in the scorching blaze of Lahore. One was young, the other was middle-aged. Their shirts were damp with sweat spreading out from their armpits, making semi-circular designs that went in all directions. They were at quite a distance, but I could still get a whiff of their sweat; the universal smell of labour class.

"Is he here? You should've called me straightaway."

Shamaila opened the glass door that led from the veranda into the main building of the house. "Come in, your highness! Why were you standing like a criminal in the dock?"

"Because I feel like one," I smiled as I followed her into the grand lobby where indoor plants and beautiful vases stood in every corner. The lobby was like a crossroads with routes spreading out to all parts of the villa. I followed her as she talked and talked and never stopped. I felt nervous at my new job and could only answer in short and brief responses.

"Saima! Saima! Your tutor is here. Professor Sahib is waiting for you in the living room!"

She was just the same at home.

"Come on Shamaila! What do you mean Professor Sahib? How do you expect me to teach her if you mock me like this?"

"Shut up! It's fine. Relax!"

The living room had an off-white carpet. I couldn't take my sandals on it, but I didn't want to take them off. As customary, socks don't go with sandals, so my feet were soiled with dirt and sweat combined. I stood at the threshold of their living room in confusion.

"Can we not just sit in the lobby? Just get us two chairs. I like to sit in open spaces."

Shamaila was clever enough to know what was going on in my mind. She handled the situation very well without embarrassing me.

"Do you know what... you can sit in the dining room. The view of the back garden is spectacular. You won't feel claustrophobic."

Saima turned to be much quieter than Shamaila. Quite the opposite in fact. She showed me her books and pointed out areas where she needed help. She looked as nervous as I was, so no other off-topic dialogue was exchanged.

We had only just looked at the syllabus when Shamaila flung the door open and poked her head through, "Dad is coming. He wants to interview you. Good luck!" She almost whispered and disappeared.

Damn! She never said there was going to be an interview. I felt my palms getting sweaty. I'd never had an interview and that too with a big-shot bureaucrat who worked at a high post in the government.

Shamaila had left the door half open. I heard heavy footsteps, and I could tell that the man who was going to walk in was wearing very expensive shoes with a solid, treated leather sole.

"*Salam,*" said the six-foot tall man dressed in a sky blue shirt, with a loud, maroon tie, light grey trousers and Oxford style black shoes. I tried to find a smile under the thick moustache but couldn't find one. His hair, dyed black-brown, were very neatly done with a side parting. I could tell he had used a very expensive brand of a three-blade razor to shave. It seemed as if he had just got ready for work, when in fact, he had just returned.

"*Salam*," I replied as I stood up. Saima stayed seated which showed that he wasn't a strict, traditional Pakistani father.

"Please, keep seated. How are you getting along?"

"We've just gone through the syllabus to see where to start…"

He looked at his watch. "When did you start?"

"Today, Sir."

He laughed as if to show off his clean and neatly aligned teeth.

"I meant what time did you start today?"

"Oh! Sorry! Six o'clock."

"So you've spent thirty-five minutes only analysing where to start."

"I know, it shouldn't have taken so long."

He smiled as if to show the deeply chiselled brackets on his cheeks that accompanied the smile.

"You don't have to explain. She's an expert in wasting time. It's not easy to handle her. She can spend an entire session every day making you think where to start. Even I don't know where to start with this girl."

This conversation calmed my nerves a bit.

"Enough for today. Have you had tea?"

"No Sir, but it's fine. Thank you."

"But I'm going to have some, so you may as well join me. Saima, off you go. You can start your lessons tomorrow."

As he drew a chair to sit at the dining table, I could already sense the aroma of tea in the air. It was very extravagant and didn't seem like ordinary tea. I could imagine the tea leaves being picked from the fields of Darjeeling or Assam; then being cleaned up, dried, packed and then shipped to Karachi. They must have travelled by air to Lahore before ending up in the grand kitchen of Jalal Ali's majestic house. His personality turned out to be as rich and towering as he was.

CHAPTER SIXTEEN

I returned from lunch with Dr Saleh and went straight to my room. I wanted to get to the part of his thesis where he had mentioned the persecuted minorities, but I didn't want to do so before my roommates went to sleep. All three of us sat in the room reading and working on assignments with very light music playing in the background. The volume had to be kept low, or we could be accused of polluting the pure, Islamic atmosphere of the campus. The *Jamiat*'s rule was simple; *anything that's fun is un-Islamic and hence prohibited.*

Salim would always be first to fall asleep. Akhtar would usually stay up late, and we would whisper as we talked about all sorts of things. But that day, I pretended to be sleepy so our discussions could be cut short. I wanted Akhtar to go to sleep so that I could get to know more about him; strange as it may sound, but I was to learn more about him through a PhD thesis.

Akhtar, who'd had a panic attack a few days ago, and who said he could even be killed for his affiliation to the strange sect, the very same Akhtar who came from the banks of the river Chenab now lay asleep in his bed; peaceful like the waters of Chenab that crawls like a huge python on the vast chest of the Punjab, heading towards the deserted lands of Sind before it submissively slides into the Mighty Indus.

I couldn't recall which chapter Dr Saleh had referred to, so I went through the table of contents to find the chapter that sounded most like it. I jumped straight to the chapter that said *Muslim Minorities in Pakistan.*

I started reading the painful history of how religion had torn my country apart. How the question of belonging to a certain sect came before honesty, sincerity and patriotism. It was sad to see how we had no nationalistic sentiment simply because religious affiliation took over anything and everything else. The nationalism shown by Muslims of India at the time of the independence movement was falsely induced in the name of Islam, and that had left behind its poisonous remnants that the society of Pakistan was still infected by. This poison had got down to the lymph nodes of Pakistan's body, and there seemed to be no cure; just a slow and painful death.

Then there was a whole page of fatwas where scholars of one Islamic sect had insisted that another was out of the pale of Islam, simply because they saw a flaw in the minutest details of their beliefs.

I read the whole chapter but never came across any mention of Quadianis. It was already getting late, and I had a long day ahead of me. Despite it being quite late at night, the ceiling and walls of our room were still releasing the heat they had stored during the day. The heat made me even more exhausted. I thought I should give up and go to sleep, but as I flicked through the pages, my eyes caught sight of numerous capital Qs on a page. I stopped and started to read. There it was! The mention of Quadianis. I went to the start of the chapter, and the title read *Non-Muslim Minorities in Pakistan.*

Non-Muslim? I was taken aback. *Are Quadianis non-Muslims?* I kept reading. I'd read the chapter before when I first read the thesis, but now, I read it in a new light.

Akhtar apparently was a staunch believer. He went for *Namaz* every time the Azan was called. How was he a non-Muslim?

The chapter narrated how Quadianis had been classed as a non-Muslim minority in the constitution of Pakistan. Dr Saleh had briefly touched upon the irony of the fact that Pakistan's was the only constitution in the world that went so far as to categorically name a sect and declare it non-Muslim.

Then there was some tedious detail on how the Quadianis believed in another prophet of their own and how this offended Muhammad's finality. This eventually left them devoid of the right to be classed as Muslims. The Parliament in Bhutto's regime had formally made an amendment to the constitution of Pakistan to take away their right to be classed as Muslim. This amendment had made the status of Quadianis a free-for-all. Their houses were looted, shops set ablaze, and many of them had lost their lives to fanatic Muslims, all because they chose to believe in what they thought was right. I was shocked to read that in 1984, Zia, the infamous military ruler of Pakistan, had gone many steps further by making it a breach of the law if a Quadiani ever chose to act or appear like a Muslim. This meant that they could not say *Namaz*, recite the *Kalima*, fast in the month of *Ramazan* and, so much so, that even have a name that sounded like a Muslim's. Committing any of these *felonies* could lead to life imprisonment and even the death penalty if the court decided so.

Then there was mention of Christians, Hindus, Parsis and a few other minorities. But the most shocking was the persecution of Quadianis because they were persecuted with the backing of the law; no other minority faced state-backed persecution.

I felt disgusted. I peered up at Akhtar as he slept. I felt sorry for him that he had to live a double life. It must be something that haunted him every moment of his life. I didn't even believe in god but was still free to move around because the law had nothing to say about me. Akhtar, on the other hand, who believed in God and Islam, was a criminal. I felt ashamed. No one should have to go through this.

The next morning, I went straight to Dr Saleh's room. He hadn't arrived yet. I would check after every lecture, and finally, towards the end of the day, I was able to get hold of him.

"Hey, Salik! Come, take a seat. Are you finished with the manuscript?"

"I haven't read it yet, Sir."

"How come? I thought you said you could get through a book in one night. You read my thesis in one night, didn't you?"

"I did, Sir. But last night I went back to your thesis again. To check on the Quadiani issue."

"Why does this issue bother you so much? They asked for it. One, they believe in a prophet after 'the'

Prophet when Muslims believe there can't be one, so the reaction is quite natural, isn't it? Secondly, Quadianis don't accept the status of a minority that the state has constitutionally provided them. That's a bit stubborn, don't you think?"

"Is it Sir? I thought everyone is free to believe in whatever makes sense."

"Well yes, in a secular state, but not in an Islamic one!"

I took a deep breath. I couldn't say much. I was confused with the whole situation. Of course I had no interest in theology, so naturally, I stopped here.

"Why aren't you worried about Christians? They too are persecuted and at a larger scale than Quadianis."

"But they don't want to be seen as Muslims. They don't want to pray like Muslims, don't have Muslim names and don't want to be associated with Islam. Don't get me wrong; I do feel sorry for Christians, especially having read the statistics about their persecution. But I feel that Quadianis are a different case altogether."

"And Shiites? They get persecuted a lot more than Quadianis. I've included some grim details about them. The total number of Quadianis killed because of their faith is not even a fraction of the number of Shiites killed since the formation of Pakistan. Why doesn't that bother you?"

"It does Sir, but like I said, the state doesn't back the persecution against Shiites. Their persecution has a very ugly side, I agree, but theirs is more of a sectarian issue. It isn't state-backed."

"Salik, are *you* a Quadiani?"

"No I'm not Sir, I swear. To tell you the truth, I'm not even a Muslim. I don't believe in religion. I don't believe in god. If I believe in anything, it's that religion brings nothing but agony to the world. I would rather die than live a lie…"

I was in a fit of rage. Dr Saleh sat back in his seat looking at me as I lost control. He was stunned to see someone declare so openly that he didn't believe in god. I had never before done so. But Dr Saleh was like a priest where I could make confessions, and maybe that's why I'd done so with great ease.

He listened to me like a priest would but didn't say whether my sin had been forgiven because he knew I wasn't asking for God's forgiveness. My confession was only to declare my belief, or my disbelief in fact, with someone at least once in my life. Reading the chapter on Quadianis had left such a bad taste that I actually felt proud of being a non-believer. Maybe this was why I had burst into rage and openly said what I said to him. Our psychology dictates our lives. Now when I reflect on this incident, I truly believe that it was my pride in being a peace-loving non-believer and not a blood-thirsty Muslim.

If a law-abiding citizen like Akhtar was to be killed only because he believed in what he believed, it wouldn't be a murder of Akhtar but the murder of a nation.

Dr Saleh remained quiet. I too, having taken all my feelings out on him, had calmed down. My heart was still racing, and I was still on the edge of my chair.

Dr Saleh smoothly changed the subject,

"Anyway, Salik! We'll talk about this later. When can I have my manuscript back?" This wasn't followed by his signature laugh.

CHAPTER SEVENTEEN

The impression of the campus on my mind had moulded itself into a mini-Pakistan. There were all sorts of people studying all types of subjects; people of diverse backgrounds. Some had migrated from other cities, albeit temporarily, to settle in the campus for the term of their course, while the locals thought that everything in the campus was first theirs and then others' because they had always lived in Lahore. Then there were two types of local Lahorites; one that came from the walled city, and the other that lived in townships outside of it. The ones from the walled city saw themselves as the custodians of Lahore because they were the true Lahorites.

Then there was *Jamiat*, the pressure group that represented the ugly side of religion that enveloped the society of Pakistan. It played the same role on a smaller scale in the miniature Pakistan I knew as the Punjab University campus. This group was responsible for anything unpleasant that happened on the campus; from student strikes to stoning the Vice Chancellor's office, to setting ablaze departments like Fine Arts where sculptures were made and this, as *Jamiat* saw it, was idolatry. From keeping an eye on who didn't offer *namaz* to torturing male students who were seen with girls was their self-styled duty; they were the custodians of everything that went on at the campus.

There were Christians, Shiites and Ismailis to represent religious minorities. But they were free to profess their faiths. Then, of course, there was Akhtar who represented the strange minority; the minority that insisted on being Muslim but was accepted neither by society nor law. But he too carried on with life, trying to avoid the trouble that awaited him at every step. He had to get a degree and so he had to remain there, whatever the cost. But he did practice his faith, albeit secretly.

The presence of Christians had never been felt in the Campus, and that too was a symbol of the Pakistani society. All sweepers, cleaners and toilet maintenance staff were Christians. That too was a true reflection of the society. Even in Faisalabad, the weak, frail, dark skinned *jamadar* who came to clean the sewage was a Christian. I remember that there was a pot put aside by the washing up area of the *haweli* which was untouchable because the *jamadar* used it to drink water. The campus hostels also had allocated cutlery and crockery in case the Christian staff had to be fed. So their presence was hardly felt on the campus, being a prototypical model of the society we lived in.

There was, though small in number, a class of Christians who had good jobs, but that was a very unusual case. A Christian was never employed as a cook in the hostels; reason being that food touched by an infidel was *haram* for Muslims who formed the vast majority of the population of the campus, just as was the case in the whole of Pakistan.

The deeper I delved into Dr Saleh's thesis, the more I felt that I always knew all this happened but had never given it a second thought.

There were rumours that the *Jamiat* goons who acted as custodians of all affairs of the campus would themselves be involved in all types of immoral activities. There were hard-core *Jamiat* guys who would flirt with girls and even call them over to their rooms late at night. I could never get my head round why girls would ever want to be in private with men whose profession was hate. But then, lust is lust and knows no bounds.

Salim regularly attended the mosque. He had many friends who were from *Jamiat*.

"How can you get along with them?" I asked him once.

"I can't. They just want to hang around with me. They need information from all departments, so they have to have informants. We have one in our department, but he's passing out this year. Maybe they think I'd be a good replacement."

"But will you be?"

"Of course not. I'm just enjoying the privileges they provide."

"Like?"

"Like watching *all* sorts of movies in their rooms, getting to *meet* girls in the meeting rooms of Hostel 12: the *Jamiat* fortress."

"You meet girls? In their presence?" I was shocked

"Yeah. It's just light talk and a bit of gossip."

"They don't object?"

"No! As long you're loyal to them!"

"And you're loyal to them?"

He laughed, "No. I told you. I'm just making the most of this time. I'm a hypocrite when it comes to dealing with hypocrites. That's my way of revenge."

I never knew Salim had depth in his personality. He was living a double life. But then maybe all of us were. Akhtar pretending to be a Muslim, me not re-vealing that I was not a believer and Salim enjoying company with girls, protected by none other than *Jamiat*, only because he offered his *namaz* in the mosque.

It shook my soul to realise that not only was the campus atmosphere a miniature Pakistan, our room itself was a prototype of the society that decayed at the hands of nothing but religion; a society that lived a double life only to be seen as Muslim. Appearing otherwise was asking for trouble.

I thought about all this in the fields that were spread all around the central mosque. I had gone there to revise for an upcoming test but got carried away with the stream of thoughts. I couldn't take them off my mind. They would haunt me all day and all night.

I packed up my books and notes and walked off to the hostel. Akhtar stood in the lobby reading a newspaper that was always securely locked up from the centre in a way that you could turn the pages but couldn't take it off the metal stand.

"Akhtar! What's up?"

"Nothing! Why?"

"Let me pick up something from the room, then let's get out of here."

I don't know what had come to my mind as soon as I saw Akhtar. I felt suffocated and wanted to be out of the campus for a few hours. With my new found wealth, I was rich enough to treat Akhtar with some good food. The two thousand rupees from Abbaji was now surplus because I knew I would get paid from tuition before the start of next month. I counted a couple of hundred rupees, locked the rest back and ran down the stairs.

I had deeply enjoyed the peace and tranquillity in the Xin Hua restaurant with Dr Saleh. I wanted to put my mind to rest so we got a rickshaw and it was soon racing towards Liberty Market in the affluent area of Gulberg.

Akhtar appeared to be as nervous as I was when I had first walked into the restaurant with Dr Saleh. It was my day to be confident, so I took the lead in getting a table and ordering food. I didn't want to spoil my upper-hand by going through the menu not knowing what was what. I remembered what Dr Saleh had ordered the other day.

"Two of 53 and one of number 12. No drinks. Just plain water."

I felt the joy in me of sounding like a regular customer.

This meeting went on up to about four hours. We sat, we ate and had a discussion that didn't seem to have an end.

"Akhtar, how can you live like this? Come on man. It must be nerve-wracking!"

"Yep! It is."

"Then why?"

"Then why?! Then what do I do? You tell me."

"Where do you go when everyone else goes for *Namaz* to the mosque?"

"I trust you, Salik, but I need you to promise that you'll keep it to yourself."

I nodded my head.

"There are another three Ahmadis who live in other hostels. One of them has a cubical, so we assemble in his room and say our *Namaz*."

"Okay. But before anything else, you say you trust me, but you never told me you're a Quadiani."

"I did Salik. I told you I'm an Ahmadi. That's what we call ourselves. That's the name of our sect. The rest call us Quadiani. We're like the untouchables. They see us as contaminated and filthy as the lowest of the low. Qadian is the name of the village in India where our sect started. I told you the very plain truth."

"I know quite a lot about you guys, but I still don't get why you deny the status of a non-Muslim minority? You wouldn't have to hide your identity if you did so, would you?"

"When I'm a Muslim, I'm a Muslim. Why should I say I'm not when I am?"

"I still don't understand your problem! What would happen if you did declare your identity as a Quadiani... or .. an Ahmadi? Why're you so scared?"

I regretted having asked. Akhtar began narrating a story. A story of tragedy and catastrophe. A story that made me despise the so-called Muslim scholars that ruled our country *de facto*. Whatever the mask, the face behind was always that of the ugly Mullahs turning the society into an epitome of evil.

I hardly spoke. Akhtar was in the spotlight. His story went on until the time we walked out of the restaurant. It was just before midnight when we got a rickshaw to get back to the campus. It was a very dark night, but that night I had learnt that our society was even darker. The roads were empty, so the rickshaw rocketed, and in no time, we were back at the campus; the campus that lived in the shadows of hypocrisy, double standards and fear. I could feel the air polluted with the stench of a rotting nation. The food stalls thrived and buzzed with loud bursts of laughter, but I felt like the atmosphere had been dubbed with the wrong track.

CHAPTER EIGHTEEN

Having tea with Jalal Ali had been a delightful experience. His personality had the air of a top brass bureaucrat on the surface but deep down was a man of great character. He was a passionate aficionado of art, music and literature. We talked about all this as we had tea in his dining room with a breath-taking view of the back garden.

The garden spoke of its belonging to the man in charge of the horticulture of the great city of Lahore. The decorum of his villa spoke even louder of the taste of this great lover of art. From paintings to the colour scheme of carpets and furniture and curtains, everything was very tastefully placed where it belonged. Sophistication is the word to describe it all.

He wasn't only a good speaker but a very good listener as well. I would only speak when he asked me a direct question, but when I spoke, he listened as if I was giving him a rare piece of information.

He had some really astonishing stories to tell. He told me of how the Chief Minister of the Punjab had called him on the very day of his appointment as secretary of horticulture. The CM wanted the vast lawns of CM House to be landscaped as a top priority.

"I told him that I had to get the Canal Bank Road in shape as a first priority, so I could either do it alongside the Canal Bank project or after I'd completed it. His reaction was somewhat peculiar, but he knew he couldn't compel me. He must've known since before my appointment that I'm a man of principle. I think he'd gambled on appointing me because he didn't seem too happy with the outcome."

It was a very pleasant surprise to know that it was he who had given the splendour to Canal Bank; the road I always felt should have been named 'The Highway to Heaven'.

"As a bureaucrat, you're always offered bribes. You can easily shun such offers from the elite class of general citizens, but it's hard to turn them down when they come from ministers."

"Then how do you turn them down?"

"I have my own ways. I have my own philosophy of life. My mother didn't know exactly what the civil service entailed. All she knew from hearsay was that civil servants were prone to bribery. But the only one piece of advice she gave when I qualified was, 'Never take a bribe. It can poison your future generations'. So I might have done favours to people but what I've never done is take a bribe."

"So, how do you avoid it?" I was still eager to know.

"When I get called to one of the palaces you know as CM House, Governor House or President House, I know something is up. So the residents of those palaces would sit and dine with me over what you can call a king's feast. Then when I'm about to leave, a butler would bring in a gift that they would present me to show how much they supposedly honoured me."

"Then how do you decline?" He just wasn't coming to the point.

"I don't decline it! I accept it. But the very next day or the day after, I send back a gift of equal, or almost equal value, I should say. On top, I place a card saying *I appreciate your time* or *please accept this token of gratitude.* That balances both accounts."

I could see he wanted appreciation. I did appreciate his tact, so I expressed my amazement on how he cleverly dealt with such sticky situations.

My visits to the villa became a regular feature, but meetings with Jalal Ali did not. I would either hear him talk to someone in the lobby or he would sometimes smile and wave as he walked past the glass panels that worked as a partition between the dining room and the lobby.

Teaching maths and chemistry to an O level student wasn't much of a big deal as I had imagined. I got on with the job very well. Saima was quiet and shy but extremely intelligent.

Shamaila asked me one day how Saima was doing, and I told her the same three qualities that I had noticed.

"And you, Little Miss think-I-know-it-all, lack all three," I had said to her before she hit me with her bag.

"Hold on! hold on!" I cried as I held up my arm to block her attacks.

"What! What is it?"

"The *Jamiat* summoned me the other day. They told me very plainly that I shouldn't be seen with you anymore."

"What? Really? And they threatened you?"

"Yeah, they did. Look, my father is not a bureaucrat; he runs a simple shop in Faisalabad. Why do you want to see me selling seeds for the rest of my life? So, stop being childish and don't ruin my future!"

"Did you not tell them my Dad's name?

"No. I don't like to hide behind other people. That's never going to make me stronger."

"I knew this was going to happen. But I can't help it. As soon as I see your face, it's like you're begging to be humiliated."

"Whatever!" I knew she couldn't be serious. "But this has to stop. We can't be seen together. Otherwise it's my head. Got it?"

"No!" she shouted and struck me with her bag one last time.

"I'm going to have to start wearing a helmet around you."

"You better do!"

She got tired, so she walked away and joined the small group of girls standing outside the classroom busy in some gossip.

I didn't know how I was going to ask for the fee to be paid at the end of the first thirty days of the tuition. I knew I would eventually get paid but didn't know how. I had imagined that Shamaila would walk into the dining room in the middle of the lesson waving three thousand rupees, slam them on the table and say, "Here you go!"

That would have been the worst scenario. Or would a butler walk in during the lesson and hand me an envelope with three thousand rupees. That again wouldn't be very decent; or would I get the money from Saima herself and wait for her to leave the room before I counted it.

But, thankfully, the fees were paid in a very sophisticated manner. I received an off-grey envelope in the post. The envelope seemed to be an expensive one; laid vellum with a majestic watermark. I didn't want to destroy its sophistication by ripping it open as I normally would, so I opened it very carefully from where the flap was sealed.

Inside, was a cheque with my name typed on top and Jalal Ali's printed at the bottom. And above the line where it read 'Jalal Ali' was a signature; what a signature it was! Like a work of abstract art made of lines drawn in one go, without lifting the pen, hastily spread all over the place.

I couldn't have thought of a tuition fee being paid in such a dignified manner. My respect for Shamaila's family increased manifold by, what was to me, going the extra mile. What impressed me most was the fact that they too must have thought about how to pay the fees. They might have thought of the ways I had imagined. Then they must have thought of a way that was most dignified.

I had to thank the family. I just had to.

"Shamaila!" I called out as everyone left the class.

"You called?"

Her expression changed all of a sudden, "Oh no! I'm not falling for... You said it yourself; *Jamiat* will drip-dry you if you're seen with me!"

"You know, if you stay serious, just this once, then maybe we can get through a full conversation."

She cackled as she held her stomach and bent backwards. After her fit of laughter, she finally got a grip, "Sorry! Go on!"

"Could you convey my thanks to your Dad? I got the cheque yesterday. I'm always impressed by his thoughtfulness."

"Tell him yourself! You come round every day!"

"Just do it! Please."

"NO! I'm not running errands for you."

And she was gone.

That evening, as I hung on the doorstep of the bus, heading to Bahria Colony, I thought how I would thank Jalal Ali. I didn't want to sound as if I was desperate for money, nor did I want to make it out like it was the first time I had received a cheque, even though it was. I couldn't draw a proper plan of action as I wasn't the only one clinging onto the footrest. It was Lahore's rush hour, and the bus was overcrowded with every passenger trying to stay in one piece. The new type of clothes I had now started to wear made me even more uneasy.

Since the day I faced embarrassment for not wearing socks, I had started to do so. And because socks don't go well with sandals, I had started wearing shoes to complement the socks. And with shoes, I couldn't wear *Shalwar-Kamiz,* so I had started to wear trousers and shirts when I went to teach, and even to the department at times. Isn't it strange, how time can change the things we think can never change?

Jalal Ali was at home. He escorted me to the dining room, talking as he walked ahead of me,

"So, young man, how are you keeping?"

"Very well Sir! How about yourself?"

"Oh, don't ask! These past few days have been hectic. So much going on that I hardly find time for the family. However, today, Shamaila and her Mum have forced me to stay at home. We're going out for dinner tonight. We'll drop you off on the way. Is that okay?"

"Yes, sure. Thanks."

"You're welcome," he said as he turned around, calling Saima to come downstairs.

"And Sir! I wanted to thank you for the cheque."

I made sure I sounded thankful but not excited. I was observing the etiquettes of talking to a man with wealth, power and character. It is difficult to find someone with a combination of all these traits.

The lesson had only gone on for half an hour when the whole family stood waiting in the lobby.

Then came the ever-fresh voice of Shamaila, "Come on, let's go. Salik, you're sitting at the front with Dad. Now, come on!"

I sat in the front seat with Jalal Ali. The three women squeezed into the backseat, with Shamaila complaining as usual,

Scoot over! Get off my shawl! Breathe the other way!

All this at regular intervals. She was, yet again, being herself.

"Is she like this in class?" her father asked with a witty smile.

"I'm afraid so. Even louder at times."

Everyone laughed as Shamaila started to tell made-up stories of how I was in class.

We approached the small bridge on the canal opposite my hostel. "Just here should be fine. Thank you."

"You know, you can come with us if you like. That's if you don't mind! I certainly don't, and I'm sure no one else does," He looked back as he asked.

"Erm… No… Actually… It's just that …" I really didn't want to go. It was their family time, and I didn't want to intrude. I would've been really uncomfortable too.

"Dad, he's going to waste time. Erm…Erm… Erm… Typical Salik. Keep going. I know he's got nothing better to do. You can enjoy his company while we talk about our women stuff."

I could see a warmth in Jalal Ali's eyes, "What do you say? It'll be good to have you with us."

"*Ajao Beta!* It'll be fun. You can teach Saima another couple of maths sums while we eat," Shamaila's mother eased the situation.

In a blissful mood, we headed off along the Canal Bank Road. I had expected to end up at a posh restaurant, but I could see his car making its way through the busy roads of the night-time Lahore towards the old city. We parked up near Anarkali Bazaar when Jalal Ali said,

"I love traditional food. I got this food street set up to bring back the traditional food that seems to be swiftly vanishing from our streets. Everyone seems to think that fast-food can turn them into Americans. They don't realise it's not only about food. Americans grew into a developed nation through very hard work before they had to invent the food that could complement their busy lifestyle. We refuse to take the same route but want to somehow get to the same destination. But it doesn't work like that, does it?"

"Of course not."

Every food stall was very busy and packed. We waited to be seated. This man, who had set up the food street, stood patiently waiting for a table. He didn't play the card he easily could have used to get priority service. He was a thorough gentleman. His family knew him all too well, so even they didn't seem bothered with him standing there waiting. They knew he was too humble to be bossy. But I was curious to see what was on his mind, so I asked,

"What if you told them who you are?"

"Hah! They would make fun of me. They might even tell me that every other customer tries this trick on them."

His wit was always sparkling.

Mustard leaves at their best: *Saag* and corn-flour *naan*. Every bite of the *naan* reminded me of Ammi's cooking. This dish was her speciality. She would cook it very lovingly, and everyone would eat it equally fondly. The food at the restaurant was good, but the *naan* was nowhere near the mark that Ammi had set. Mothers have a unique ingredient they add to everything they cook: the invisible ingredient of selfless love.

CHAPTER NINETEEN

No matter where I was and no matter what I was doing, Akhtar's mysterious story remained etched on my mind. Although the apparent feeling was of sympathy for a fellow countryman living in fear and not being able to exist freely, the undercurrent was the pain that I felt for my country that was at stake. History alone is sufficient to tell that such societies crumble and eventually turn into ruins.

Akhtar had spoken at length to describe what his family had been through. He would have to pause intermittently to compose himself. He choked on many occasions and wept at others.

He told me that his brother Hamid was a student at the Allama Iqbal Medical College in the very city of Lahore, not far from our university campus. He was in his final year in 1984 when the ordinance of Zia came out, prohibiting Ahmadis from not only calling themselves Muslims but also doing any act or using any term that could make them resemble a Muslim. This, practically, could mean anything. The law had been so vaguely drafted that it could be taken to mean anything and it *was* taken to mean anything, not only by the Sharia courts of Pakistan but the general public also. It was widely publicised, and Maulvis would openly declare that it was every person's duty to ensure that Quadianis were not seen performing any act that made them appear a Muslim.

Akhtar went on to tell me that his father was a shopkeeper in Rabwah, where he sold groceries. They could hardly make ends meet. Ever since Hamid was in school, his parents had made Hamid work hard in studies and assisted him in every possible way to gain entry to a medical college. The family would have the bare minimum for meals as they saved up for Hamid's private tuition which could enable him to get the grades required. He finally got very good grades and was offered a place in Allama Iqbal Medical College. The entry fee and the monthly cost of living in Lahore were beyond their reach, so his mother had sold all her jewellery that she was given as a custom for her marriage. This was to materialise the dream of their son becoming a doctor. But even then it could only generate an amount sufficient to pay the entry fee and the fees for the first year's study. They knew it would be a long journey with the course spanning seven years. The parents had no idea how they would carry on fostering their life-long dream after the first year, but they continued to save up for the next instalment and then the next.

Family meals had become even simpler and had been reduced to two a day. The entire family realised the gravity of the situation but never complained. But the savings were not enough. Akhtar's mother started sewing clothes for women who didn't possess the skill. This would get another few hundred rupees on top of their father's earnings. Children tradition-ally are not told much about problems that parents go through; they try and keep it to themselves.

But their house was very small. A kitchen, a bath-room, and one bedroom. Akhtar would sometimes overhear his parents and get an idea of what they were having to go through. They would talk secre-tively about how much had been saved and put aside. Then they would sometimes talk about buying a plot of land; then also about building a house on the plot. He would often think how on earth they would buy a plot and start building a house when they didn't even know how the existing expenses were to be met. But it wasn't for him to fix their accounts, so he didn't interfere. Neither did any of his siblings as it wasn't acceptable for children to have a say in such matters.

It wasn't just Hamid that took all his parent's attention, all siblings were encouraged to work hard in their studies so that they could secure a better life than their parents.

They would save all year round and then give Hamid their savings to pay his college fees. The day they handed him their savings would seem to be the happiest day of their lives. The poor couple would rejoice and celebrate the day by cooking something good for the whole family. It would be one day in the whole year that they got to eat some good food, but that too was rationed.

Time passed by and they continued to pay the fees year by year.

They knew he was doing well at college because he would get promoted to the next level every year. They never demanded anything back from him. The only one thing they always insisted on was that he should be regular in his prayers and never to forget to recite the Quran.

"Whatever we've been able to do for you was a result of prayer. Do you think someone like me with a small grocery shop could even imagine sending his child to a medical college?" Hamid was always told this by his father.

"And don't forget to read the Quran!" His mother would never forget to add.

Every Mosque in Rabwah had a system where they would inculcate the skill of understanding the Quran. They were encouraged to ask questions and were made to grasp the meaning. The Maulvis at the mosque emphasised that Quran primarily taught two things: love for the Creator and love for the creation. They were told from early childhood that Jihad did not mean to wage war against peoples, but it was a struggle against one's own self; not falling into temptations. Those lessons at the mosque had made Akhtar get through every test of Islamic studies in school and college. He would usually do even better than the 'certified' Muslims.

Hamid was brought up in this atmosphere. He never missed *namaz* and was often seen studying the Quran. Like all others in the town, he was pursuing secular education but had a deep understanding of Islamic teachings.

The day his parents paid off Hamid's final year's fee was the happiest day of their lives. They had bowed before God many times that day, and night, in gratitude. They had achieved their biggest goal yet.

But what they did not know was that this final year had actually brought some surprises for all of them. It was 1984, and the Anti-Ahmadiyya law had come out. They were not fully aware of the extent of its impact. They had thought it wouldn't affect common Ahmadis like them and would be restricted to the Ahmadi press and publications. Hamid had taken the early morning train from Rabwah to Lahore. His father and mother had seen him off while the other siblings were still in bed. It seemed like the usual start of an ordinary day. But something quite the contrary lay ahead.

A boy who worked at the shoe store near his father's shop had come running.

"It's a call for you. From Lahore. They say it's urgent," the boy ran back. Akhtar's father dragged himself as fast as he could, not even shutting down his shop. The shoe shop was only a few yards away. Not everyone had a telephone in those days. The majority were poor and couldn't afford to have one. So the number his parents would give to friends and family was of the shoe shop. But a phone call would always bring bad news. Otherwise, no one really bothered to pay for an inter-city call for good news.

"Hello *Ji*," Akhtar's dad said, trying not to sound out of breath.

No one knew what was said from the other end. Those who had witnessed later told that the receiver just slipped out of his hand. He stood still and silent in shock. He didn't say a single word and just walked with heavy steps back to his shop. He stood there for a minute looking at his shop from the outside. He put on his sandals and walked away, leaving the shop unmanned.

Everyone around rushed to ask if everything was alright. He stood quietly. He seemed stunned. Then he silently walked home.

Akhtar and his family had never seen his father come home so early. He would normally shut his shop after the late evening *namaz* and would return home after dark.

Akhtar's mother had asked if everything was alright,

"I don't know!"

"What do you mean you don't know? You've gone pale. Are you okay?"

"I am. I'm okay. But I need to get to Lahore. Now."

"Lahore? Why?"

"I've been told that I will have to bring Hamid back."

"Tell me what's happened! Why bring him back? What did he do? Can you please tell me what's going on?" His mother shouted.

"He hasn't done anything. But I've got to bring him back."

"Who called? What did they say? They must have told you more. He only went this morning! And what do you mean 'bring him back'?"

"I just have to!"

He just gazed at the floor. It seemed as if he was trying to avoid eye contact.

"Beta Akhtar, call Khalid Uncle from next door. Tell him to come and speak to your father. He's lost his mind! Go quick."

Khalid Uncle had entered, almost running.

"What happened *Bhai Ji*? Is everything alright?"

"Yes. Everything is fine. Can't you see everything is normal? Do you see something wrong with me? I'm fine. Let me go. I just need to bring my son back!"

"But why *Bhai Ji*?"

The whole family was perplexed. They looked at their old father sitting on a chair, staring at the floor as he said things that didn't make sense.

But when he came back to his senses, he spoke. But as he spoke, he broke down. He lost control,

"What do you mean why? Don't you want to mourn him? Don't you want to bury him? Don't you want to see him for the last time? Our Hamid is dead. He's no more!"

His father wept dreadfully loud; so loud that he didn't even have the energy. After a few loud wails had drained him, he murmured, "I just want to bury him with my own hands; my dear young son with these old, frail hands. Let me go. Let me go."

Akhtar's mother fainted and collapsed. Uncle Khalid's family and other next door neighbours gathered to see what the screaming and wailing was all about. Everyone ran to attend to his mother, as his father talked on, as if to his own self.

"They killed him! They killed him just because he was reading the Quran in his room. They killed my son. My Hamid is dead because he had the book of Allah!"

His tone wasn't clear. It had sorrow, astonishment, disgust and pity; a strange amalgamation of all.

The next door neighbour had driven Akhtar's father to Lahore along with some family friends. Hiring a van to bring the body back was beyond their capacity, so the local carpenter had happily offered his. Bereavement and what follows is not dealt with as systematically as one would expect in the western world.

His body was brought back and laid to rest. Everyone in the college had a different story to tell but what was common in all versions was that Hamid had arrived in the hostel and gone to his room. A mob of students had been asking for him in the hostel and was waiting for him to arrive back. Having ensured that he had returned and was in his room, the mob had raided his room. They were heard yelling,

Why do you have the Quran in this room? How dare you touch it? Bloody Kafir! You insult the Quran by reading it! You insult the Quran by touching it!

They had brutally beaten up every limb of Hamid's body. He screamed in pain, but the beating went on. No one moved forward to help; they knew it would be asking for trouble. Trying to help a Quadiani was as bad as being one, so the hostel inmates crowded outside at a safe distance until the point when Hamid's screams could no longer be heard. The mob could still be heard yelling, swearing and raising slogans, but Hamid's cries had died, and so had Hamid.

Having made sure that the mob had left, the hostel administration had called an ambulance. Hamid's badly bleeding body was taken to the hospital and then to the mortuary; he had succumbed to severe head injuries. The police had arrived but had refused to register the case. The ordinance was fairly new, and they didn't want to end up doing something that could land them in trouble. Law enforcement agencies were oblivious of how to register the murder case of a Quadiani citizen of Pakistan.

His poor parents had to see their dream buried before their eyes. They had approached the local police station who had said that they could register a case, but there were chances that the law might want to go into details of how he had got the Quran, why he had it and who had given it to him. The police officer had said that there was a chance that his father could get booked for providing him with the Quran. So the case was not pursued any further. His father had no energy left to defend himself in a fabricated lawsuit. His mother agreed, helplessly, to not pursue it any further. She didn't want to lose any more loved ones to a law that was inhumane if anything.

His parents lived on as mere bodies without souls. However, they continued to invest their meagre resources and desires in Akhtar's future, who was now their only son. Akhtar had discussed the option of quitting education and helping his father in earning a living. Both his sisters were yet to be married, and that meant hundreds of thousands of rupees to prepare their dowry, jewellery and the paraphernalia of Asian marriages. But Akhtar was strictly told not to even think along these lines and carry on working hard with his studies, which he did.

He didn't know how his parents would fund his education because their savings were now buried in a grave with a headstone that said 'Hamid Mahmood 1959-1984'. But Akhtar was astounded to find out from his mother that the plot they had bought and the house that had been built on it while Hamid was in college was rented out and had been generating funds to fuel Akhtar's university fees.

So Akhtar was now their only hope and couldn't afford to make the same mistakes as his elder brother.

I had often seen Akhtar standing on the balcony of the hostel, gazing towards the building of Allama Iqbal Medical College which was only a few hundred yards away, across the fields that lay in between; the very place where his brother had been ruthlessly murdered for being a Quadiani.

CHAPTER TWENTY

Coming back from the traditional dinner I had had with a very untraditional family, I felt that it was not a waste of time after all. Jalal Ali's company was never a waste of time; one always learnt a lot. But the tragedy is that the more you listen to inside stories of the Pakistani society, the more disgusted you feel.

I saw their car drive away as I walked on the Canal Bank towards my hostel. I thought about what they would do when they got back home. Full of life as they were, I couldn't imagine them being tired and lazily lying around the house. But I also had to think about what I was going to do when I got back.

I felt tired, but I had to read the manuscript of Dr Saleh's book.

Akhtar and Salim were not in the room. I knew they would be around killing time or may be saying *namaz*.

I took the manuscript out of my cupboard and removed it from the large brown envelope that had absorbed the smell of the adhesive glue on the flap.

'Pakistan: The Bedrock of Global Terrorism'

Wow! What a bold topic.

No wonder he had strictly instructed me to keep it carefully away from anyone else. I started reading it. I was more comfortable with my roommates now and knew that they wouldn't be nosy about what I was reading.

I continued to read even when Akhtar and Salim walked in, one after the other, from wherever they had been.

As an unsaid agreement, we wouldn't disturb anyone who was trying to read, so I managed to continue in peace.

Dr Saleh had touched upon very unconventional and sensitive topics like the blasphemy law of Pakistan. He must have known that he was playing with fire, but he was very honest in expressing what he thought. He had examined the ridiculous law which, in practice, meant that anything could amount to blasphemy of the Prophet.

He had quoted a news report from a few years back where a woman had argued with a rickshaw driver on overcharging her for a journey. The woman had pointed to his beard saying, "You've grown such a long beard, but you're still ripping people off!"

The driver had taken his asking amount and driven off. After an hour, the police had come knocking at her door and charged her under the blasphemy law for mocking the beard which, as the case read, was a practice of the Prophet.

A Christian priest had been booked for saying *Lord Jesus, Saviour of the world,* because this, according to *an* interpretation of the blasphemy law, undermined the status of the Prophet.

A Student of Islamic studies in Peshawar University was arrested as a result of a tip-off from his fellow student that he had asked a question about the many marriages of the Prophet.

In all of the cases quoted, the general public had killed the accused even before the courts could decide their fate. The woman who 'mocked' the beard was poisoned by a female staff of the prison; the Christian priest was shot dead while being driven to court for his initial hearing; the student was beaten to death during the interrogation at the police station.

Dr Saleh had very rightly pointed out the fact that out of the three, only the priest was a non-Muslim, the other two were Sunni Muslims and, hence, from the largest Muslim sect of Pakistan.

Then there were thousands of cases registered against Quadianis for using the salutation for the Prophet that is incumbent on every Muslim to say whenever the name of the Prophet is mentioned, in speech and writing, both. Some Quadianis were arrested under the blasphemy law for merely including *hadith* of the Prophet in publications. To my surprise, a Quadiani was trialled for reciting a poem praising the Prophet. *Islamic law took the praise of the Prophet of Islam as blasphemous? How strange!*

I read the whole manuscript overnight. Dr Saleh had concluded by agreeing with many academics who were of the opinion that the root cause of the extremist tendencies that had evolved into global terrorism lay in the writings of Maududi. Another bold claim that Dr Saleh quoted from many academics was that almost all terrorist organisations formed in the name of Islam had stemmed from the anti-Quadiani agitation that had happened in 1953, almost adjacent to the formation of Pakistan.

The next morning, I held the manuscript very carefully close to my body as I walked from my hostel to the department. I went straight to Dr Saleh's office but saw that he was attending some guests. I wanted to hand him the packet before I went to the lecture room. He took the packet and asked me to see him in the afternoon. "Before lunch!" he winked. As he said this, I knew I was having a nice meal again.

As we sat for down for lunch in Gulberg Grill House, I asked.

"Sir, are *you* a Quadiani?" He knew I was returning his joke.

"No, I'm not! I'm only a human being. I am not pious enough to belong to any religion."

This was the first time Dr Saleh had confirmed the doubts I had always had. It is a fact that anyone who talks sense in Pakistan is usually a non-believer or is declared a non-believer for talking sense. Pakistani Islam had no room for sense and sensibility.

"But you've brought the whole issue down to the anti-Quadiani sentiment!"

"It's not about Quadianis, it's about the truth. When a state starts targeting a certain section of their society, this is what the result will always be. The state becomes a party in the case and loses the equilibrium that is essential for the smooth running of state affairs."

"But Sir, you said Quadianis too are to be blamed, didn't you?"

"Well they are, but that's a theological debate. I'm not a theologian to settle those differences."

"What *is* the difference, by the way?"

"Well, the difference is all based on nonsense. All Muslims believe that Jesus Christ will appear in the latter days. Quadianis believe that he has appeared. Now they get accused of taking someone to be a prophet after Muhammad, but the fact is that all Muslims are waiting for a prophet after Muhammad. In my opinion, there's absolutely no reason to declare them non_Muslims. And if I'm brutally honest, I've found Quadianis to be better persons than many Muslims."

"So what's the problem?"

"I told you I'm not a theologian! I don't know what is right and wrong in theology. Apparently, I don't see anything wrong, but my argument is that anyone can believe whatever they want. They want to believe there is a prophet after Muhammad, let them. They think Muhammad was not a prophet, let them. Someone wants to believe in Muhammad to be the last prophet, they can do so. But no one, even the state, should have the right to force someone to believe in something and not in another."

"So what's the way out? You've analysed the whole problem but without a solution."

"Don't ask me to do everything. As a social scientist and a student of political philosophy, I can point out what is politically wrong. I can't take the onus of everything on me. I've done the diagnosis, now let someone else find the right treatment."

"And where do you see all this heading to?"

"Disaster! Chaos! Annihilation!"

"Then, what's the way out? I mean I know you want someone else to work on it, but what's your personal stance?"

"Take religion out, and everything will be fine. Europe was stuck in reverse gear until it left religion aside to be a matter of personal choice. We want to be like Europeans but don't want to take their route to success. The church ruled Europe just as Muslim Mullahs rule us today. They had the same problems; extremism, sectarian violence, persecution of religious sects and everything bad that religion is giving us. There is nothing wrong with religion as long as you leave it to be a personal matter. The moment you use it as a tool for political power, it loses substance and leaves behind a swamp that keeps swallowing the society."

"Substance? Does religion have any substance at all? I thought you just said you don't believe in religion!"

"You jump to conclusions too soon, don't you? I don't believe in the formal forms of religion that we see around us. I have a spiritual side. I believe that there is a creator because not believing in a creator is as unscientific as believing in a set of rituals that make the Creator happy."

"Why is it unscientific to not believe in a creator?"

"Because then you're being as rigid as the fanatic believer. He says that there *is* a creator because he thinks so, and you say that there *isn't* one because you think so. You're both aboard the same boat then, aren't you?"

"But there isn't sufficient evidence to prove that there is a creator!"

"Neither is there sufficient evidence to prove that there isn't!"

"Then why believe in one?" Now I felt like I was defending a faith.

"Then why not believe in one?" Dr Saleh was becoming difficult.

"Because there's no outcome?" I still stood firm.

"Well, this is for an individual to determine the outcome. Those who aimed for a good outcome of religion eventually achieved it. Those who determined a corrupt outcome eventually accomplished their goals. The section of the society you and I want to change does not represent religion. They represent oppression and fascism. No founder of any religion used it as a tool for political control."

"Muhammad did?"

"No, he didn't. He was a prophet and a statesman at the same time. He ruled the Arabian Peninsula but used his religion to find ways of forgiving, to find ways of implementing law and order. Even if he used religion to enforce the law, he wasn't wrong. We forget that he was introducing law and order to a society that had been lawless for centuries. You're a student of political science. You should read the *Covenant of Medina*. I'm sure you'll change your mind."

"I don't think I will!" I replied quite firmly.

"Then you're no different than a fascist Maulvi, I'm afraid. Why don't you join *Jamiat*? You'll feel right at home. They are exactly the same. They're rigid and will only believe what they want and yet not let others believe what they want."

This heated debate could go on forever, but Dr Saleh suddenly cut in before I could respond,

"Well, this has been great! I love debates, but I love my family more. They're waiting for me. Shall we carry on some other day?"

"Sure, we'll settle this later."

"We sure will," replied Dr Saleh, as we walked to his car.

CHAPTER TWENTY-ONE

As soon as you start to settle in campus life, time begins to fly. MA was a two-year course and the first year had already passed. The second and the final year was more demanding than the first. We had five papers to take at the end of this year, and the sixth paper was a dissertation that we had to write to qualify.

I had proposed to write my dissertation on *Religious Minorities in the Constitution of Pakistan*. I had submitted the proposal to be considered by the department's Board of Studies. This was a routine procedure, and all students had to go through it.

Ghulam Rasool came looking for me in the library and told me that Dr Amin Uddin wanted to see me in his office at one o'clock in the afternoon. I had had the chance to attend a few lectures that he delivered from time to time but had never got to meet him in person.

I nervously waited outside his office as the peon went in to ask him if I could be sent in. The wait wasn't too long. The peon came out and ushered me in. Dr Amin Uddin was seated at his majestic desk, most of which was neat and tidy. Only a couple of books on his right-hand side with ornamental pen holders, a calendar with polished wooden blocks with names of days and dates on them; souvenirs from European countries and decoration pieces took the rest of the place. On his right side was a shelf with a few books stacked on either side to make the mostly empty shelf not appear uninhabited. The spaces in between the books spoke of the hollowness of the shelf and of the person who owned them.

"How have you planned to write this?"

"I've mentioned in the synopsis that ..."

"I know what you said in the synopsis, but I want to hear it from you. Your synopsis isn't as clear as to let me know how you're going to attempt this topic."

He sounded quite stern and straightforward.

"I plan to analyse the constitution and see how our politics regarding minorities are governed by it."

"How?"

I didn't know what to say. I wasn't ready for this interview.

"Erm…. Maybe by looking at the minority-specific clauses …"

"Maybe? You've proposed a topic, and you still aren't sure how you're going to take it further?"

"I mean… I meant that…"

"You aren't sure because this topic isn't directly related to political science. This is more for a law student to write on than a student of political theory. I feel you should change the topic. Go for something more straightforward. Submit a new topic and a new synopsis."

He pressed a button somewhere under the table to ring the peon's bell who stepped in and held the door open. The meeting was over.

"Thank you, Sir," I said as I walked out. He didn't make any eye contact or even bother to reply. I walked out, totally puzzled. *Why wasn't my topic relevant? Why was I called to be told that I had to change my topic? I thought it was the most relevant one. What else could be more relevant to the politics of a country than its constitution?*

I went straight to Dr Saleh's room. He wasn't there.

"Ghulam Rasool! I want Dr Saleh's phone number immediately," I said as I stormed into the department's main office.

"Calm down! You know the protocol; Order a cup of tea, and I get his number out."

"Oh come on man! Give me his number! You'll get your treat. His number?"

My mind was sizzling as I dialled Dr Saleh's number from the telephone booth at the main campus market.

His wife picked up and said that he had gone to Islamabad and would not be back before the following Tuesday.

"Is there any way I can contact him. Any number?"

"I don't think so. He's staying in a hotel. I don't have any number. I'm Sorry."

The conversation had been very brief but enough to cause further distress. He was the only one I thought would understand and put up my case with the Board. Five long days lay ahead before I could tell him what I was being put through and how unfair this was. I had no choice but to wait.

I went straight to my room. Final year students were moved out of dorms and were allocated cubicles, so it was good that I could be on my own.

"What the hell! Bloody nonsense!" I spoke to myself as I banged the books on the table and threw myself on the bed. After about fifteen minutes of solitude, I felt that I had to talk to someone. Even if no one could help, I had to just get it off my chest.

I got out of my room and walked down the balcony that led to Akhtar's room. He had also just got back.

"Akhtar, let's go!"

"Hey! What's up! Where to?"

"I don't know. Let's just go. Anywhere but far away from here. Come on man, quick."

I didn't even let him change. We got out of the hostel and walked straight to the rickshaw stand at the main gate of the campus. We didn't say a word as we walked to the rickshaw stand. I didn't know where to start, and Akhtar knew that it wasn't a very good time to ask.

We jumped in the first rickshaw at the head of the queue.

"Lahore Fort!"

I don't know why I said this, but the rickshaw had raced off in no time.

I looked out as the trees, buildings and people walking around flew past our speeding rickshaw.

"*Salam* Sir Ji! How is your mother?" The driver asked

I looked at the driver's rear view mirror to see a familiar pair of eyes.

"It's me, Abdullah. I dropped you off at the coach station about a year ago. Remember?"

I did remember, but I was in no mood to start an unending talk with him.

"Yes, I remember. My mother is fine. She's a lot better. How are you?"

"I'm fine. Thank God your mother has recovered. My wife prayed for her. I told you her prayers get accepted!"

In the mood that I was in, this was enough to tick me off.

"Abdullah! Why doesn't she pray that your circumstances change? Or does she like to see you driving a rickshaw in extreme weathers, puffing all this polluted air all day long?"

Abdullah had got me at the wrong time.

"What else shall I do? We're all happy with what we have. All our happiness has come from this rickshaw that I drive. It's because of this rickshaw that I was able to get my two daughters married and my son into a decent school who'll be going to college next year. We eat simple food, but we love it. Nobody is appointing me a minister if I left this rickshaw. And even if someone offered, I don't think I'd go for it. I am happy with the way I am. I'm thankful to Allah."

These believers are impossible. They always seem to have an answer even if it happens to be an illiterate rickshaw driver.

"This Allah of yours, why did he write in your fate to be a rickshaw driver? The rich and wealthy sit in their homes as money flows in, while you're on the road all day sweating your socks off to take a small amount home every night?"

I was completely pissed off. Or maybe I wanted to piss him off, but he remained unmoved and very happy with his god.

"I don't care. I don't think everyone is as happy as they seem. And also, I don't think everyone is as unhappy as we sometimes imagine. I'm happier than many. Sir Ji! You can't imagine how my wife's face glows with joy when I hand my wife the hard earned money every evening!"

"Okay, as you say," I decided to drop it here. It wasn't getting anywhere.

"But you look worried Sir Ji! When Mother is healthy and all good, what else in the world could worry you?"

Our worries are defined by what we are. For a rickshaw driver, the biggest worry could be an illness of a family member and the expenses it can incur on the bread winner.

"Nothing! It's some university matter. Something to do with my studies. You won't get it."

"Okay. Allah help you, Sir *Ji*," Abdullah had solid faith in Allah.

"I don't think your Allah is in any mood to help me." He set me off again.

"My Allah?" he smiled as he repeated.

"Yes. I hope you don't mind?"

"No Sir Ji! I don't mind. I love my Allah. Some don't love their Gods. We all have our own ideas about God."

I looked at Akhtar in surprise. He knew why I was looking at him, so he smiled back and raised his hands as if to say, *I've never met this guy. I didn't feed him all this!*

As we got off outside the grand entrance of the Lahore Fort, I asked Abdullah how much we owed.

"A hundred, Sir *Ji*. It's the same. The coach station is just across the road, so it's the same as ..." He started to give explanations for which I couldn't care less. I handed him a hundred rupee note, thanked him, and we walked off.

We had only walked a few steps when we heard the noise of a rickshaw very close behind us. I turned to see Abdullah smiling and following us. I stopped and asked as I approached him.

"Now what?"

"I wanted to give you your change," he said as he held out a five rupee note.

"Change? I thought I gave you the exact amount," I said, slightly confused.

"Sir Ji! Something is bothering you. You're worried. Give these five rupees in charity. I'll ask my wife to pray for you."

"Abdullah! I don't believe in bribing god. I don't expect him to change my circumstances only because I gave him a small amount of money. Don't worry. Just keep it!"

"I can't Sir Ji! I've already made the intention for it to go to charity. I can't contaminate my day's earning by putting it back."

"Okay," I said helplessly. "Then give it to charity yourself. And thanks anyway."

"No Sir Ji!"

This guy just wouldn't let go.

"You're worried. You give it yourself, so that the one you give it to, prays for you directly. I don't want to come between you and 'your' God," he laughed as he said this. His pale eyes, stained teeth, scruffy shave, everything joined him in the joke he'd cracked.

I took the money from him, looked around and gave the money to a beggar I spotted nearby.

The beggar said prayers for me and my non-existent relations like my wife and my children.

"Akhtar! I bet this driver is related to you!"

Akhtar burst out with laughter, "Why? Because he makes sense? Because he left you and your theories speechless? Well done!"

It was a pleasant spring afternoon in Lahore. Lahorites had come to the fort for excursion. Some families sat on the grass in small groups having a picnic. One could tell that hardly any family was bothered about the history of this fort where they sat in groups having *samosas* and *pakoras*. All they knew was that summer was now just around the corner, and they had to make the most of the spring before the sweltering sun torched the city. The sky was full of colours as kites flew around as far as one could see. The kite festival of *Basant* had only just passed a few weeks ago, but then no one could take out the spirit of festivity from the soul of Lahorites.

I told Akhtar what had happened that morning. I knew he couldn't do much about it but to console me. He agreed that it would be a good idea to speak to Dr Saleh about the issue and fight my case with the board.

"If I do manage to get my topic approved, I would want to visit your town and interview some officials of your community to see how they see the anti-Quadiani laws. Sorry anti-Ahmadi laws," I quickly corrected myself.

"Sure! Anytime! You'll be more than welcome."

CHAPTER TWENTY-TWO

I had been going to Shamaila's place for over a year now. Her dad would sometimes send me a message through Saima or Shamaila that he would see me after I had finished. I would then make my way to the sitting room where I would sit and wait for Jalal Ali to arrive. He would always come accompanied with the waves of knowledge, power and control. I would look forward to meeting him. I would sometimes stay for dinner when invited.

It was one such evening that I had a meeting with him. I knew he wouldn't be able to do anything, but I was adamant to tell him how the proposal for my thesis was being treated by my department.

"But why would you pick such a topic?"

"It's our constitution! It carves the way for our politics. What's wrong with it?"

"No, nothing wrong! It's just a bit slippery, that's all. Your department head was right. This might be asking for trouble, and your department might get a share of it."

"What trouble?" I was totally baffled.

"Don't you know where this could lead to? You would be treading on areas that are taboo; no one goes down those lanes anymore. Government agencies keep an eye on dissertations that get written in universities. Anyone picking such topics could end up being questioned. And when you have *Jamiat* ruling your university, the likelihood of you being spotted is extremely high. Try to pick something more straightforward."

"Fine. Agreed. But what's wrong with the topic? I want to explore, and I want people to find out. This could be a step towards change."

"And that's exactly what they don't want!"

"Who are 'they'?"

"The ruling class. It's like an unsaid agreement between anyone who comes to power and the right-wing extremists, that issues like blasphemy law and minority affairs would not be touched and left as they were."

"Why would a government be obliged?"

"Because they want to stay in power. There has to be a class among the citizens that has to be discriminated to enable the ruling class to prove their loyalty to the state religion. Any fascist regime has to have one. Jews were targeted in Germany on the grounds that it was the Jewish financiers who had led to Germany's disaster in the First World War. This gave Hitler a ground to prove his nationalism and patriotism through persecuting the Jews."

"But it wasn't only the Jewish financiers who got killed in the genocide. Any Jew could be killed."

"That's right. But fascist regimes always base their foundations on a certain proposition, then the proposition gets diluted in the course of events. Masses are made to believe that living up to that one proposition is the only way to prove loyalty to their nation or religion. The agents of fascist regimes work on strengthening the general belief that sticking to that dogma is essential. If they didn't, they could be punished either by the state if the cause was political, or by both God and state if the cause happened to be religious."

"But which religion? Do you really think these rulers of ours have anything to do with religion?"

"They don't, I know! But the proposition has to be kept alive to maintain their control. The masses stay occupied in proving their loyalty to the proposition making it easier for the rulers to rule them.

The masses drain all their energy in sticking to a dogma and are left with no potential to use their own minds. This makes it easy to maintain control and exercise power."

Now I had an interesting situation. A government official sat there telling me how the government controlled the masses' minds.

"You know, I thought you would tell me not to withdraw my proposal. I actually thought you might encourage me to stick to it and get it approved. But now I understand. You too have to prove your loyalty to your employers." I smiled, so the satire didn't sound too harsh.

"I work for the Government, but I don't have to agree with their psyche. There has to be a government, and there have to people who work for them. A civil servant is employed by the government, but at the end of the day, he's a servant of the people. I don't like to make emotional decisions. If everyone starts to quit the civil service, there would be no one left to serve the public!"

He always had a philosophy behind his ideologies.

I left their house but was undeterred. I knew I was going to go ahead with my plans anyway. I wasn't about to give up, without a fight.

The following day was the Tuesday when Dr Saleh was due back. I wanted to call him first thing in the morning, but then I thought that having travelled all day, he might have been tired. So, I decided to call him later in the evening.

When I called, he picked up in his usual way

"Hello, Dr Saleh speaking!"

"It's good to finally hear your voice, Sir. I wanted to know if you'll be coming to the department tomorrow?"

"Unfortunately I won't. Why?"

"When will you be in next Sir?"

"Erm. I might not be in for some time. Why do you ask? Is everything alright?"

"I don't think everything is alright. How can I meet you, Sir? I need to sit down with you to discuss something really important. At this moment, only you can help."

"Okay. I should be home all day tomorrow. No, hang on, not all day. How about you come and see me around eight o'clock in the evening."

"Sure Sir, I'll look forward to it. Thank you. *Salam*."

I couldn't wait to inform Akhtar of my newfound knowledge; what went on behind their persecution. Jalal Ali had opened new avenues for me to understand why there existed a discriminatory tendency in fascist governments and societies like Pakistan. I went to his door and knocked, but there was no response. I asked the gatekeeper if he had seen Akhtar around. He said that Akhtar had left straight after classes.

"Did he say where he was going?"

"No one bothers telling us," the gatekeeper simply replied before taking a long puff of his cigarette.

I wanted to tell Akhtar that his community was not just being persecuted. There was a gruesome scheme behind it. I wanted to give him the bad news that the fear his community faced would remain as long as the ruling class didn't find an alternative substance to intoxicate their masses with.

I wanted to share the grief that would strike his heart when I told him that there seemed to be no such opium seen even in the distant horizon. He, and his community and other so-called *non*-Muslims would have to become scapegoats of this so-called Muslim society for many decades to come.

I searched for Akhtar at Rafiq's stall, in the campus market, in his department, in the cafeteria but he was nowhere to be seen.

I walked back to my room in despair.

CHAPTER TWENTY-THREE

The next morning, I didn't feel like attending classes. I wanted to talk to Dr Saleh before I could go back to Dr Amin Uddin. And I wanted to go back to the department only when I had spoken to him and had my proposal approved.

I caught a shuttle that ran between our campus and the old campus of the university. Both these campuses were miles apart. The old campus was the building that originally housed the University of the Punjab when it was first established by the British Raj in 1882. The majestic building was on The Mall: the heart of Lahore. Most of the buildings on The

Mall stood as a remnant of the time when the British had thought they would never have to go back and had invested a great deal of funds and skills in erecting buildings that had both, a Victorian feel and an Oriental touch. The Lahore Museum, Dyal Singh Mansion, Jinnah Library, Laxmi Mansions, Government College, the General Post Office known as GPO, the Cathedral of Lahore and the Punjab University all told stories of an empire where, once upon a time, the sun would never set. The story of their past glory all concluded on the fact that the sun had set in this part of the empire and the buildings stood aghast in the long, dark night that had stretched itself to the present day.

As my sight caught the cathedral, an idea flashed. I thought I should go in and ask if I could speak to some official of the cathedral and get an insight into their understanding of the laws that discriminated them. The traffic was at a standstill, so I hopped off the shuttle and started walking towards the cathedral. As I stood at the main gate of the cathedral, I looked back at the road. The traffic hadn't moved an inch. I thought that if I wasn't let in, I would just run back and get on the shuttle again. I rang the bell on the grand pillar of the gate. *Once, twice, thrice.* No reply. I was about to run back when I saw a man coming out from the grand, majestic door of the cathedral. He wore a very pleasant smile as he approached me.

"How can I help you, Sir?" the middle-aged man asked in a very polite tone. He wore green trousers and a white shirt. He had lost most of his hair from the top of his head but had covered his bald patch by growing the hair that had somehow survived on the sides and laying them across. This hairstyle had always fascinated me. *Do they really think people won't know they're bald?*

I could smell my favourite Tommy Hilfiger scent from his clothes. His shoes were as shiny and tidy as they could be on the dusty roads of Lahore. That meant he didn't have a car and either walked to the cathedral or used public transport. I imagined him sitting, or standing, in a bus. *Could passengers around him tell that he wasn't from among them? Did they know that he was different from them?* I thought that no one could ever tell he was different to Muslims unless he told them about his faith. Why does a small statement make us alien to others when there is nothing in appearance that makes any difference?

"Hello Sir, I'm from Punjab University. I'm writing a dissertation on the minorities of Pakistan. I was hoping to see someone in this regard."

He smiled as he listened. "Do come in. Let me see if there is anyone available to help you, but even if there isn't, I can offer you a cup of tea if you like."

"Sure! Thank you," I said as I walked with him to the main building of the cathedral. I turned back to see that the university shuttle still stood where I had left it.

"I'm Joseph. Joseph Bhatti. And you?"

Trying to hide my surprise at the fascinating combination of his names, I introduced myself in detail; in good time before we were in a large reception room. By the reception room, was a fully functional office. Men and women were busy working. Their laughs and cackles, their conversation and the noise of the typewriters all combined to make the typical music of a busy office. It was the same in offices where Muslim staff worked. All the staff looked like normal human beings; nothing different except a belief that sat in the heart. But our society didn't want a belief to stay where it belonged. We wanted people to wear their faiths on their sleeves to know whether they deserved to be first class citizens or one from the second or the third classes.

Joseph brought me a glass of water and asked if I took sugar in my tea.

He disappeared again through the small door that led to the office. He came back very soon and invited me to walk with him into one of the offices that were on either side of the corridor that ran past the reception and went on to end at a big double-door that opened in the main assembly area of the cathedral.

"Hello! I'm Oscar Shahid. I work for the press and information desk. How can I be of assistance?"

"Thank you very much for your time, Sir," I said before I explained the reason for my visit. I told him that I was already working on the dissertation rather than tell him that the matter was still under consideration and I was being asked to withdraw my proposal. I was careful in saying anything to him when I found out that he was the man in charge of the press and information. I did not want to be misquoted. I had some regret of having just walked in before the topic could be approved, but there I was, sitting with this gentleman, telling him what I was after.

"You must be very brave to have taken up this topic. I'm surprised you actually have been allowed to work on this. I don't think your department would be happy or are they?"

"They seem fine with it," I lied plainly. "But even if they didn't approve, it wouldn't bother me. I really want to know how you as Christians see the whole situation and how the constitution affects you."

"As far as the constitution is concerned, it doesn't affect us much. The wording seems to be very protective of us. It's just that the blasphemy law, in practice, can be exercised on us in any way that one pleases. We could be in breach of the law even if we said in a service that Lord Jesus was the King of the world. Even professing that he was the most beloved man ever to have lived in the world would mean breaking the law of the land."

"Why do you continue to live in such a land?" I had always wanted to ask someone from the minorities, and today I had got the chance.

"That's a good question! Well, because this land is our homeland. We made sacrifices for this land just as much as anyone else. Our forefathers lived here, we earn our livings here on this land, this is where our children were born, and this is where we all belong. It's as much of a homeland for us as it is for anyone who lives in this country."

I could feel the passion that throbbed in every word of this statement.

"Of course, Sir! I appreciate that."

We spoke for about an hour or so. I was shocked to learn how vulnerable such citizens of my country were. Oscar had offered me to see him anytime I wanted. I was extremely thankful to him for this.

I was escorted to the gate by Joseph. He saw me off in a very pleasant manner. I didn't know what to do next.

I walked across the road to the Punjab Public Library, trying to find material on the topic. Everything I came across was written by foreign authors, and I could sense that their knowledge of the topic was shallow. No one can have a true feel of the situation unless they live or have lived in Pakistan. There was no complete work dedicated solely to this topic, but it was scattered here and there in small passages, mostly as passing statements.

Some liberal Pakistani analysts like Barrister Hamid Khan had touched it in *The Constitutional History of Pakistan*, but there was nothing to suggest the gravity of the situation. I noted down the names of the books that I thought could come in handy if Dr Amin Uddin was kind enough, or courageous enough, to grant me permission to proceed with my proposal.

I wandered off to the *Baghe-i-Jinnah*, previously known as Lawerence Gardens before it got Islamised at the hand of Mullahs. It had been a good decision to bunk classes as the day had proven very productive. I had had the chance to speak face to face with members of a minority and the peace and quiet to think about how I would go about my dissertation if it was approved.

It was approximately Seven O'clock when I caught the bus to head to Model Town, Bank Square where I would get off and walk to Dr Saleh's house.

CHAPTER TWENTY-FOUR

I had come back very late from Dr Saleh's house the previous night. I got out of bed to take a shower and head to the department. Dr Saleh had told me what to do next. He wasn't going to be around for a fairly long period of time, but he had said that Madam Atiqa should be able to help.

"She's like you! She doesn't believe in God. She'll be happy to help someone from her own community." This was followed by his signature laugh. Dr Saleh couldn't help joking even when things got serious.

As I rushed off to the department, I thought I should check on Akhtar. I knocked on his door.

There was no response, but I knew that he always left for his department at about quarter to nine. It was nine o'clock then, so I knew that he would have left.

The day ahead proved to be a very hectic one. Dr Atiqa listened to my proposal very carefully. She told me categorically that the department would never accept it. There was too much pressure on the department not to endorse any views that seemed to be directly aimed at the constitution. The constitution was like a gospel for the ruling class, which they had no respect for but had to show that they did. They claimed to believe, based on certain interpretations of the Quran and Hadith, that the constituent assembly actually exercised a divinely given responsibility when it drew the constitution of an Islamic state. Dr Saleh had also told me this much the previous night.

She advised me to make certain alterations in the wording of the synopsis for the proposal to be accepted by the board. She happily gave consent for me to suggest her name as my supervisor so that it could be materialised. This was the only way this thesis could slip through the tight net of my department's scrutiny.

She proved to be very cooperative. She let me sit in her room to revise my synopsis. She would go for her classes and then come back and check what I had done, suggesting further changes. Every change she suggested was enough to prove the depth of her knowledge on the subject. I was glad that there had finally been a solution to my problem, but I still had my fingers crossed as there was still a chance for the board to uphold their previous decision.

I wrote a cover note and submitted my revised proposal to Dr Amin Uddin. I had no idea what the outcome would be and when I would be informed about it, but I was very hopeful that Dr Atiqa's presence would make a difference as she had promised to fight my case to her best. Questions could also be raised on why I had changed my proposal about the supervisor. But even there, we had a leg to stand on because Dr Saleh was going to be away for a fairly long time.

It was now a matter of wait-and-see and no other choice.

I went back to my hostel hoping to find Akhtar. I had always wondered how we sometimes knew if someone was inside a room without even having to look inside. I had a feeling that Akhtar was not in the room even before I knocked. I knocked again and waited, but all that came back was silence and nothing more.

I ran down to the gatekeeper. It was a different gatekeeper's shift than the one I had spoken to the previous day.

"Have you seen Akhtar?"

"Which Akhtar? The one from Chiniot?"

"Yes!"

"No, I haven't!"

Now, I was alarmed. I ran to his department to check if he had attended classes during the day. I asked a group of students busy gossiping on the staircase that led to his department. They hadn't seen him and weren't sure if he had been around. I went to his department's office to check if he was marked as present on the attendance register. He wasn't.

I ran back to my hostel to ask Salim. Although all three of us had moved out of the dorm into our own separate cubicles, we were still very good friends. He wasn't in his room, but a friend of his told me that he had gone to the cafeteria with a group of friends.

"Who were they? From his department?"

"No. They were from *Jamiat*. He often goes out with them."

My next destination was hostel 12. I ran as fast as I could but stopped at the gate. The aura of that hostel was different from other hostels. There were no gatekeepers. *Jamiat* thugs worked in shifts as gatekeepers of their hostel. They spotted me running towards the hostel but then stop suddenly. That perhaps wasn't a very wise signal.

"Come here!" one of them shouted intimidatingly and approached me faster than I was walking.

"What are you up to?" he said sternly.

"I was … I am actually looking for Salim from Geography department. Someone said he'd come this way."

"Oh! Salim *Bhai*. Wait here."

He went back to the gate and shouted out to someone inside.

"Tell Salim *Bhai* there's a visitor who wants to see him."

The person on the other end said something which I couldn't grasp. But the reply from this end was quite clear.

"Check in 45. He should be there."

It took a good ten minutes for Salim to walk out of the hostel gate.

"Salik! What's up? What are you doing here?"

"Sorry, Salim! Sorry for the trouble. Do you have any idea where Akhtar is? I haven't seen him since yesterday, and he wasn't in class today. I'm getting a bad vibe!"

"He's fine. He's gone home."

"Home? Chiniot?"

"Yes! Chiniot! Come on in. Let's have a cup of tea."

"No. I'm good, thanks. It's good you told me about Akhtar! I was starting to get worried."

"Why? Why were you worried about him? Didn't you think he might've have gone to Chiniot?"

"Well, no, because it's not like him to disappear without telling me. Anyway! I don't know why I was worried. But, yeah, you're right! I should get going now. I guess I'll see you in the hostel later tonight."

"I'm not be coming back. I've moved here. I'm in room 45."

"You've moved here? Why's that? I thought you said …"

"Doesn't matter. We have to make compromises in life. But it's fine. I know what I'm doing. I'll come and see you soon, and we can have dinner someday at Rafiq's."

"Sure. Done."

Although I didn't show it, I was now more concerned for Salim. No one could just move into the *Jamiat* hostel unless they proved themselves worthy. What had Salim put himself into?

CHAPTER TWENTY-FIVE

When Salim came to see me, I had just got back from my department. It had been a long day with so much going on. The final year was much more hectic than the first year had been. Too many assignments to be submitted and too much coursework to get through. I felt I wasn't comfortable with Salim anymore, but here he was offering lunch at Rafiq's stall.

The food was good, and good food always tastes even better when you're hungry. I didn't know where to start, but Salik seemed more confident than ever before.

"So what's been going on? It's been a long time since we sat down and talked!" He started the conversation.

"Yeah, you didn't even bother to tell you were moving to Hostel 12."

"It all happened so quickly that even I didn't realise what was going on. My friends from *Jamiat* came and told me they had got a room allocated for me there. They made me pack all my stuff so that I could move out. I just couldn't resist."

"Why couldn't you resist, Salim? Even in my wildest dreams, I couldn't imagine visiting a hostel which was the fortress of *Jamiat*, let alone moving in and living there all day and night."

"I told you, we have to make compromises. And besides, it's only giving me advantages and doing me no harm. They want information, and I provide it. That's all. And by the way, they only promote an Islamic way of life. I too believe that that should happen."

"Promote an Islamic way of life? Through torture? Through terror? What kind of Islam is that?"

"Well, you see, even the law has to enforce itself through penalties. Islam is a code of life, and once you claim to be a Muslim, you have to live up to its standards, or else, the law enforcement can come into action."

"Who is *Jamiat* to define Islamic law and to enforce it?"

"Their claim to establish an Islamic society is enough to give them the right to do so, don't you think?"

"No! Not at all! I don't think so."

It was a disappointment to see Salim promoting the *Jamiat* agenda, knowing that *Jamiat* was nothing but hypocrisy. He had told stories of what went on in Hostel 12. He knew full well that they promoted what they didn't practice. Salim had been the only one I could share my worries about Akhtar with, but that was no longer possible.

The following day was Friday. I went to Akhtar's department to try and get hold of his contact details but didn't know how to go about it. I knew no one there. Salim could have been a great help in getting hold of Akhtar's contact details but not anymore. His new Islamised version could actually be jeopardising Akhtar's safety.

I went to my department and spoke to Ghulam Rasool. I took with me a bag full of *samosas*.

"Here you go Ghulam Rasool! You always complain about me not meeting your demands. This is all for you and your staff here."

"Why, thank you. Now tell me what you want!" Ghulam Rasool seemed very happy as he said this, dipping his hand in the bag of samosas.

He rang the Philosophy department. All the clerical staff in various departments seemed to know each other too well.

"The guy from Chiniot. Akhtar." He explained to the clerk on the other end of the phone.

"Really? Do you want to double-check?" He paused for a couple of seconds, covered the mouthpiece of the receiver with his greasy fingers and looked at me as if to say something, but then decided not to.

"Go on!" He said as he started to scribble something on a piece of paper.

He had finished noting down the details, but I could see that the clerk on the other end was talking to him. Ghulam Rasool listened attentively, but with concern, something he never did. He always had too many comments to make and would hardly ever let you finish your sentence.

He put the phone and the samosa down and signalled for me to follow him out of the office.

He took me to the side and looked around to see that no one was listening.

"Why do you want to contact him?"

"Well, he's my friend. A very close friend. Why?"

"He's not your friend. Otherwise, he wouldn't have lied to you."

"Lie about what?"

"About who he is!"

"What are you trying to get at Ghulam Rasool? Come to the point!"

"If he was your friend, he would have told you who he was and where he was actually from. He isn't from Chiniot. He's from the Quadiani headquarters: Rabwah. I would urge you to stay away. His conspiracy has been caught halfway. *Jamiat* is looking for him, and so is the department. So it's best you stay away."

"That's bullshit. Tell me the truth! What's going on?"

"This guy was planted in the university on a Quadiani assignment. I don't know the details, but what has been discovered so far is that his plans got uncovered halfway. The department is trying to contact the police and *Jamiat* are doing what they can to get hold of him."

I paced down the stairs. I was heading to Akhtar's department to see what had been going on. As I approached the main corridor from where smaller corridors led to various departments, I noticed a procession outside the philosophy department. They held placards with Akhtar's name, demanding his arrest and for him to be put to justice.

Wipe Quadianiat off the face of Campus!
Quadianiat No More!
Akhtar Quadiani, Death Awaits You!

I made my way through the roaring mob of *Jamiat*, trying to reach the office upstairs.

The office was locked from inside. I knocked, but no one opened. I thought I should proceed to the lecturers' rooms past the department's clerical office, but a guard stopped me in my steps.

"Sorry, Sir Ji! You can't go this way. I have orders that no student can go past this point."

"Get out of my way. You guys think you can stop people like me; try and control the mob downstairs if you can!"

I tried to push him aside, but he resisted, telling me not to move a step further or else he would call the police.

The commotion right outside the department office led to a clerk opening the office door.

"What is Akhtar? What did he do?" I turned to the clerk who took the one step back that he had taken forward.

"Go and ask the mob downstairs. They'll tell you," he said, as he locked the door again.

I ran downstairs. The mob was now ready to proceed to the Vice Chancellor's office, shouting even louder than before. Newspaper reporters and paparazzi had started to gather around the mob. A spokesperson was giving an interview to the handful of reporters from private television channels and newspapers. I tried to get closer to hear what he was saying, but the mob wouldn't let me get anywhere nearer.

I ran off to my hostel to see if there was any coverage of the events on the television. Newscasters were breaking the news of a Quadiani plot foiled in the new campus of Punjab University. They were constantly trying to get in touch with their reporters at the campus but were failing to get through. The reporters were probably still trying to get connected.

I switched between the many channels that all earned their livings from such stories. To break the news first meant good ratings, so the newscasters were desperate not to let viewers switch to another channel and were constantly claiming that they had got in touch and that their reporter would soon give a statement, live from the scene.

One of the channels finally got through to the reporter. By now, a huge crowd had gathered in the hostel lobby, around the television. Students, kitchen staff, gatekeepers, cleaners and waiters all gathered before the screen to see what someone from their very own hostel had been plotting to damage their country.

The reporter started off at the top of his voice so that he could be heard amidst all the noise of the mob in the background.

"Viewers, we are here at the new campus of Punjab University. Behind me is the Vice Chancellor's office as you can see. And you can see the mob that is protesting against the university administration that has refused to cooperate with them in filing a case against a Quadiani who posed as a Muslim and got enrolled at the University under a Muslim name and Muslim identity."

"What do we know so far about this student? What was the conspiracy?" the newscaster interjected.

"It's said that the Quadianis are planting their youth in universities with Muslim names and identities who then work on executing the Jewish plans of corrupting the minds of innocent Muslim students in colleges and universities. A Quadiani called Akhtar Mahmood enrolled himself in the Department of Philosophy here at Punjab University. He had been trying to convert innocent Muslim students to join him in his activities. The undercover Quadianis who posed as students would assemble in a room in the Sir Syed hostel in the new campus about three to four times a day. A tip-off led to their plot being foiled …"

The newscasters wanted to bring him to what the viewers would want to know.

"Are you able to tell us what the plot was? What's the conspiracy?"

"That has not been disclosed as of yet. *Jamiat-e-Tulaba-e-Islam* says that it would not be in the nation's interest if the details were revealed before a case was registered against them. They are pressurising the philosophy department to file a case against Akhtar Mahmood with the Muslim Town Police Station, but they've refused to do so as they do not have any firm ground or evidence. The mob has now proceeded to the VC's office to mount pressure on the VC to register the case. The *Jamiat* spokesman has said that should the university refuse to do so, a case would be filed against Akhtar and his associates by every single member of the JTI. That could potentially mean a few thousand cases being filed against the Quadianis in question who are all at large. Ali Faruqi with cameraman Asim Chaudhry, reporting from new campus!"

"Thank you, Ali. We now move on to Maulvi Sanaullah, an Islamic scholar who needs no introduction, he is live with us on the phone. *Salam.* Maulvi Sahib?"

And then the Maulvi told viewers how the Quadianis had always been an enemy of the state; they had never left any stone unturned in trying to tarnish the name of Pakistan; they served the Indian agenda, the Jewish conspiracy and that they were planted in Pakistan only to assist the western powers in annihilating Islam and Pakistan. He said that if a case wasn't registered, it would be justified to kill them if they were to be found anywhere.

The entire lobby was filled with murmurs. For those living on the campus, it was the most sensational news that anyone had ever heard because they had met the culprit many times. Akhtar's photo was shown on the screen every now and then during the news bulletins. Everyone in the hostel was dumb-founded to know that the student being shown on the screen, who looked like an innocent young lad, was actually a criminal in disguise, plotting to bring their country to destruction. Some were disgusted to recall how they'd had food with him when it was actually *haram* to have food with Quadianis.

I turned around to walk out of the lobby where ignorance was at its height. I felt sick to my stomach. Everyone I bumped into gave me strange looks. Those that had the courage made stupid remarks.

He would've known. They were always seen together!

He'll know where they are. They always knew each other's whereabouts...

As I ran up the stairs, I bumped into Salim who seemed to be in a terrible rush. He was panting.

"Salik! I came to see you. You need to get out of here! You're next. *Jamiat* knows that you were close friends with Akhtar. Go anywhere, but leave this area now!"

"Salim!" I wanted to ask so many questions, but Salim just ran down and out of the hostel. I rushed straight to my room. I didn't want to be seen carrying a bag around. That would make me look suspicious. So I didn't take a bag. I stashed all my money from the lockable drawer and my ID card in my pockets, and I shoved Dr Saleh's thesis in the drawer that I had just emptied and locked it securely. As I walked along the canal, I could see that the campus now looked more like a crime scene. *Jamiat* henchmen were crawling around with megaphones declaring a strike and ordering all departments to shut down. *Any department found functioning will be set ablaze!* It looked like scenes from a military coup. Students had walked out of their departments and were trying to get taxis and rickshaws to get home before things got really out of hand. Police sirens destroyed the peace and serenity of the campus. Ambulances rushed through the main gates. I walked as fast as I could to the rickshaw stand. The queue of rickshaws outside the campus was distorted. Drivers had all come out of their rickshaws trying to get a safe-distance view of the panic and chaos.

I walked closer to the drivers.

"Abdullah!" I shouted out loud as soon as I caught sight of him.

"Abdullah!"

"My friend!" he came rushing to me and jumped in his seat, pulling the lever to start the engine of his racketing rickshaw.

"Quick Abdullah! Take me to the coach station, please!" I said as I held on tight.

Abdullah felt lucky that he would be the only one to come back and report a first-hand account of the commotion. He asked curiously what had happened. I didn't know what to say because I didn't know what to believe; how to tell him that the guy that sat in his rickshaw the other day was accused of being a traitor, a terrorist and an enemy of the state conspiring against Pakistan.

"They're accusing a Quadiani from within the campus of treason. They say he posed as a Muslim…."

Abdullah listened silently. I could see only his eyes in the mirror. He seemed to be in deep thought but didn't ask questions.

"God have Mercy!" he said with a sigh and drove on.

I took out a hundred rupee note as I got out at the coach station. Then I added another twenty rupees.

"Abdullah, thanks for getting me here so quick. Take this; the extra twenty rupees is to give in alms. Give it to someone in need? And also ask your wife to pray for the situation!"

Abdullah stared at me, then at the money in his hand. He didn't know what to do. He seemed unusually quiet, but I could sense his concern. He kept the twenty rupees note and gave me back the hundred.

"I'll give this in alms. You keep the hundred. You get a third ride free in my rickshaw." He attempted a smile and handed back the money.

"Look, Abdullah, I don't have time to stay here and argue. Keep it! Just keep it!"

"Sir Ji! I hope you return safely. I'm not having this money. *Salam!*"

He turned his rickshaw drove off having squeezed the money in my top pocket.

I got a seat in a coach that was going to Sargodha, via Faisalabad. I bought my ticket and an evening tabloid newspaper. Akhtar's photo took up most of the front page. *AKHTAR! What have you done!* I was certain he wasn't a criminal. As I sunk into my seat, all I could think of was my good friend, who was the most loyal among any friends I'd had in my life. I felt helpless as I thought where he could be; what his poor old mother and father must be going through. I could only imagine their agony as they had lost their eldest son in the same way that her second and only son was now nearing. I could only but feel for them. I felt so helpless.

I sprang up from my seat.

"Will this coach go straight to Sargodha from Faisalabad, or will it stop en route?" I asked the conductor

"We briefly stop at Chiniot."

"How much more if I want to get off at Chiniot?"

"Another fifteen rupees."

I gave him another fifteen and continued to read every line of the newspaper. It had the strangest details to report about Akhtar's case.

My ears caught some comments flying around at the coach station about the Quadiani terrorist that had been conspiring against Pakistan in the university.

CHAPTER TWENTY-SIX

The coach had left Lahore at around two o'clock in the afternoon. I got off at Chiniot at approximately twenty to Six. I went straight to the ticket kiosk and asked for a ticket to Rabwah.

"The coach doesn't leave for another hour. You'll be better off getting a rickshaw and crossing the river," advised the salesman at the kiosk.

It turned out to be a cheaper option because the rickshaw driver took as many passengers as he could and they all shared the fare. I had to pay only five rupees, and we were soon crossing the river to get to the other side. All other passengers on the rickshaw were going to Rabwah. They seemed like normal human beings. As normal and innocent as Akhtar.

The journey was really short and quick. The rickshaw dropped us all off at the main road. I was a complete stranger there. All other passengers made their way into the town called Rabwah as I stood looking around, thinking what to do next. I was soon approached by someone standing by who had been watching me from a distance.

"Are you alright?" the man dressed in *Shalwar-Kamiz* asked politely but firmly.

"Yes. I'm actually here for the first time… to see a friend… but I don't know where he lives."

My answer made him appear more suspicious of me.

"So, he invited you but didn't give you his address?"

"Actually … what it is, is that …"

"Does your friend have a name? Or did he forget to tell you?"

The situation was getting trickier than I had thought.

"His name is Akhtar. I'm his friend from Punjab University."

This left him expressionless. I now felt that I was taken to be suspicious. He turned back and gestured to someone to come over. It was as if the other guy was already waiting. I felt like I was standing at the border of a country waiting to be cleared by the customs and immigration control. I stood there recalling that Dr Saleh had mentioned in his thesis that Quadianis allegedly had their own state within the state. I now thought that the allegation wasn't too wrong. I did feel like I was seeking entry to a different state.

The person guarding his town now stood before me accompanied by three men, one of them armed. All of them looked well-built and towered over me. I was told that I would have to go with them to their office while they tried to trace Akhtar.

I climbed into their jeep. I felt very uncomfortable with the type of welcome I had been given at the Quadiani headquarters.

I was soon seated in a small room of an office. I was told that someone called Aleem would see me shortly. Aleem looked more decent and educated than the men that had escorted me here.

"*Salam.* I'm Aleem. I apologise for the strange welcome you were given. I hope you can appreciate that our town is constantly under threat. We receive threats literally every day, both against residents and the town. The majority of the residents in our town are Ahmadis. This is the only place we can live relatively more securely, and we try to guarantee them a bit of security in this small town. So don't be offended."

"Of course, I understand," I said so because I actually did understand their position.

"So you are...?"

"Salik. Salik Qadri."

"So, Salik, you're Akhtar's friend. You know what he's going through. Because of that, we'll have to ask him if he is okay with seeing you. At the moment, we can't ensure how safe it is for you to see him though. I don't mean at all that we have any doubts about you, but we have to have his consent. I hope that makes sense?"

"Of course it does. Tell him it's Salik from his hostel."

I sat in the office as Aleem walked out of the room. I felt more comfortable now that I had met a friendly face. I could totally understand why they had to put their security measures on high alert. I sat as comfortably as anyone would at border-control, understanding that the measures, albeit unpleasant, were completely justified.

I could hear Aleem talking to someone on the phone giving a statement on the situation.

It must be some foreign channel because Pakistani channels never gave Quadianis the chance to express their viewpoint, I thought as I overheard the conversation.

He came back after a few minutes. He told me that BBC's Urdu Service had called to get his statement. So I knew that he was a spokesperson for the

Quadiani community. That gave me a chance to tell him more about myself.

"I'm actually writing a dissertation on how religious minorities are discriminated with a backing of the state. I had spoken to Akhtar about visiting Rabwah someday and speak to someone like yourself and get your angle of the situation. I just didn't think my first encounter would be like this."

He said that he would be very happy to talk to me about it anytime.

We spoke at length at what had happened all morning that day on the campus. How Akhtar had been accused of treason and how the mobs had been pressurising the university administration to file a case.

"My sources have told me that the VC has refused to launch a case, but the pressure is still mounting. It's likely that the university will have to give in."

I was surprised to see how well-informed he was.

One of his staff walked in to say that food was ready. He led me to a dining area within the compound. The way the food was served showed the respect they had for their guest, who still remained suspicious.

After food, I was shown the way to the restrooms and a guest room in case I wanted to rest. I didn't know what was happening and didn't want to ask. I knew that they were aware of my presence and that I was waiting to hear if Akhtar had acknowledged that it was safe for him to meet me.

"You can rest a little if you want while we say our *namaz*. You're more than welcome to join us," said Aleem, with a rather welcoming smile.

"Thanks. I think I'll wait here."

"That's okay, I know you can't offer prayers with Ahmadis."

I couldn't tell him that that was not the case and the fact was that I didn't offer *namaz* at all. I was in a dilemma. I didn't want to give them the impression that I wasn't offering *namaz* with them because I thought they were Quadianis. The detail of why I didn't offer *namaz* could sound like an excuse more than anything else.

"Do you know what... I will join you. Let me just freshen up, if that's okay with you."

"Sure. We'll wait for you."

I came out of the bathroom to see about nine people in a line, waiting on the prayer mats. One of them led the prayer. I was surprised to see that a guy wearing jeans and T-shirt led the prayer as the Imam. I never knew you could qualify for leading *namaz* without the typical Maulvi-attire and a full-length beard. This version of Islam was new to me. It seemed more welcoming and more acceptable.

I was quite used to pretending that I was saying *namaz* but this experience turned out to be completely different.

It all started off as normal. I was familiar with some of the verses that were being recited. They were the ones that Ammi made me memorise and revise every night before going to bed as a child. Maulvi Sahib at the mosque would sing the same verses.

It was my first-hand experience to notice that the Quadiani prayer was said in quite a Muslim manner. I continued to sit, stand and bow with them as I peered around the office. As my gaze wandered around, I noticed I was the only one doing so. Everyone seemed to be in a trance. I felt their suffering.

They were a community living a life of insecurity in my country; in their own country actually. Their agony had left them with no other choice but to submit to an unseen power to come into action and grant salvation. They had tried all visible powers and were left with no choice but to turn to an invisible one. I could see that they were trying their best.

When the prayer was over, a guy standing on duty nearby told us that Akhtar had arrived. I was told to sit in the room where I had previously been sitting with Aleem. I thought it would only take a few seconds to get there because the entrance of the office wasn't far from where I was seated. But it took much longer than that.

I was now alone in the room waiting for Akhtar to walk in at any moment. I anxiously looked at the clock every minute, so I must have looked at it around fifteen times.

Eventually, Akhtar walked in. We didn't say a word. We were both curious, concerned yet confused. I couldn't utter a single word to console him. We didn't know where to start.

"What's going on Akhtar?"

"You tell me! You're a student of politics. You tell me what's going on 'cause I don't have a bloody clue."

"Something must have led to all this. Where do you think this ignited!"

Akhtar looked right and left.

"Let's go to the guest house and talk. I'll tell you about the conspiracy that I'd been cooking."

We were driven in the same jeep that had brought me to the large complex. I was told that it was a guest house to accommodate any visitors from outside the town. To my surprise, it was like a grand hotel with residential rooms, a dining area and a lobby where guests could sit and talk or watch television. Akhtar was given a key by the guy who had escorted us in the jeep. He took me to a room where there were a few sofas. We sat down by the window. I could see that Akhtar was trying to think where to start. He was extremely worried. A case of treason would usually end up in death penalty at the most and life imprisonment at the least.

I had to jump start the conversation.

"So! What happened?"

"Nothing happened. It's just bad luck I guess. I think someone must have noticed that three other Ahmadis and I would assemble in the same room at the same times every day. The assembly time usually happened to be *Namaz* time. Everyone would walk to the mosque while the three of us would walk to the Ahmadi's room in Sir Syed hostel. We would say our *namaz* there.

"Then, one day as we walked out of the room, the gatekeeper called me and asked me random questions, like if I knew such and such person? I told him I didn't, but he said he was just wondering because I looked very much like him. Then he asked where I was from? I told him that I was from Chiniot.

"The next morning, I was called by the department office and asked to confirm my address. I looked around carefully to check that there was no one who could hear and told him my address in Rabwah; the same address they had in their records. I asked why they wanted to confirm my address and the clerk said they were only updating their records.

"I had a feeling something wasn't right, so I mentioned it to the three other Ahmadis later in the afternoon. They said that the same had happened to them. I thought that it could be linked to the dialogue I had had with the gatekeeper. The rest confirmed that the gatekeeper had been nosy with them also over the past few days.

"We all agreed on the chance of something being planned against us, we decided to flee and get back to Rabwah as soon as possible, until the situation was clear. That's all. I swear to God, that's all that happened. We fled for our safety and nothing else. Now, whether this is a conspiracy or not, I don't know."

"But Akhtar, it's strange you never talked to me about it!"

"We took no time in making a move. We went straight to our rooms, packed what was necessary and left. We didn't even leave the campus together. We left the campus through different routes at different times. But what the hell has happened to everyone? I just can't get my head round all the crap that's being spread? You know me, Salik, I couldn't even think of being involved in such stupidity."

"Of course I know you. I can say I know you well enough to be certain that you could be anything but a traitor. Things have been a bit strange over the last few days."

I took a deep breath before telling Akhtar, "Salim has joined *Jamiat*...and ..."

"What! Are you serious! Salim? Why? And *Jamiat*?"

"I don't know. I hated him for doing so, but he said that he was doing it just for fun. He said he wanted to treat hypocrites with hypocrisy. And to be fair, he actually lived up to it. It was Salim who told me to leave the campus as soon as I could because *Jamiat* was going to get me if they couldn't find you."

"Does Dr Saleh know about all this havoc? What does he say?"

"He must know by now because it's all over the news. I met him a few days ago. He took study leave and is leaving for the US in a few days' time. He is as vulnerable as you are because his upcoming book speaks in very loud tones about your community and how it's being persecuted. The book actually covers all minorities.

"But the truth that he hasn't told anyone is that he applied for a study leave only as a cover. When his book launches in a week's time, he will have left Pakistan. He knows there's going to be a lot of hue and cry about it. His life would be at risk here. If it goes to this extent, which it most probably will, he will then resign from the university and settle in the US. His book is being published by a top-notch American university. He's an established academic and that too in a very specialised field. Any university in the US would take him on board very happily."

"So you too are at large?"

"Supposedly so!" I smiled and saw Akhtar a little less distressed than he was when I had first seen him about an hour or so ago.

"So what will you do now?"

"I don't really know. I was thinking of calling Salim, but I don't have his hostel number. And he lives in Hostel 12 now!"

Akhtar thought it wasn't safe to call the hostel from a Rabwah number. It was very easy to trace it back if they were to stoop any lower which they most surely could. He suggested that we should go back to the security office and discuss the situation with them.

CHAPTER TWENTY-SEVEN

When I called at Shamaila's place, she picked up the phone.

"Salik! Where are you? Are you alright?"

"Yes! Why what happened?"

"Don't you know what happened? Your dodgy friends have landed you in trouble. I always knew you hung around with stupid people. You got branded as a traitor because of your friends. *Jamiat* is looking for you everywhere. They came to me asking if I knew where you were …"

"So, what did you say?"

"I said I didn't know because I didn't. You didn't even bother to tell me."

"Shamaila, I need you to calm down. Is your dad around; I need to talk to him?"

"No."

"Well, when he gets back... when does he get back?"

"He said he was going to be late. He should be back by ten. Now tell me, where are you?"

"I can't, at least not right now. And don't tell anyone I called. Even if they pressurise you, just keep quiet."

"Okay. You aren't telling me where you are, what would I tell them anyway? Can you..."

"Shamaila, tell your dad it's something important! I need to speak to him! I'll try calling later tonight. Bye for now."

I hung up. I wanted to call Salim. Only he could tell me what was going on in the campus.

"Aleem Sahib, can I please get the number of hostel number 12 of the new campus?"

"I'm sure you can. But it won't be safe to call from here. Why? Who do you want to call?"

I told him, and he agreed that it could be vital information that we could get from Salim, but calling the hostel from a Rabwah number could be too much of a risk. It was decided that we would go to Faisalabad and call from there. We were on our way to Faisalabad, but Akhtar had been made to stay behind.

We got off the main road near Allied Hospital and stopped at the nearest phone booth.

It was a task and a half to get hold of Salim. But luckily, he finally came to the phone.

"Hello."

"Hello, Salim don't say my name. It's Salik."

"Oh! Mr Qadri, How are you?"

"What's going on?"

"Great! That's good," he was speaking nonsense.

"Salim. What's going on there?"

"Yeah, sure. Hostel number 9. Okay, yeah. 10 minutes."

I got his message. He couldn't take the risk of talking to me from where he was. In ten minutes time, I called hostel number 9. Salim picked it up and told me a story that sent chills down my spine.

The university had declined to file a complaint with the police. *Jamiat* had decided to continue protesting and individually file cases against the four Quadianis who were at large. They wanted them to be arrested and brought to 'justice'.

Jamiat was looking for me also and carrying out inquiries here and there. Salim said that they didn't seem too furious about me but only wanted to know if I knew anything about Akhtar's whereabouts and his conspiracy. He insisted that I shouldn't have gone into hiding and that I should try and get back to the hostel so that the level of suspicion on me could decrease.

"They're pressing me to give them as much information about you as I can. I didn't have much to give anyway, so I've only told them that all I know is that you're from Faisalabad. But I don't think to flee the scene was a great idea. Come back and speak to them." Salim sounded firm in his stance.

The university would remain shut for an unknown period of time. *Jamiat* had positioned their men to ensure that no department was functional during this strike. It was like curfew in the campus, and the students who hadn't managed to leave the campus were too scared to even move around. The whole place was deserted.

It was almost half past ten when I finished speaking to Salim. It was more of a one-sided conversation; he would only tell me what I needed to do. He had asked where I was, and I said I was in Faisalabad.

I decided to call Shamaila's dad from there as it would have been too late if I had waited to get back to Rabwah.

He was home and advised me to travel back to Lahore and get straight to his place. He said I could stay at his place for as long I wished. I had the feeling that he didn't want to talk about the whole issue on the phone. After all, he lived in a government's colony.

When we arrived back at the guest house, it was almost midnight. Akhtar was waiting for me in the room, and we were roommates once again after many months. We speculated about the situation and watched the news channels where the story was no longer the pressing issue but would pop up from time to time, whenever a channel got hold of a Maulvi who could spice up the stale story and confirm that *Jamiat* was right in taking direct action if the university refused to do so.

"What do you plan to do next?" asked Akhtar as we finally got sleepy in the early hours of the following day.

"I think I'll go to Lahore tomorrow. I want to speak to Jalal Ali who works in the high ranks of the Punjab Government. I'll try and see if he can help in any way."

"I don't think he will. It's too risky. No one wants to dip their hands in it."

"I'm sure he will. But even if he doesn't he'll give some good advice. Where do you see this going? What usually happens to Ahmadis who get booked in false cases like this?"

"I can see myself being arrested and being sent to jail. Many Ahmadis are sitting in jails waiting for their fate to be announced. Even when we try and get the judge to reconsider and tell them that there was no evidence for the allegation, the

Maulvis take stay-orders before the verdict is given. Judges are changed on every hearing so that our cases lose coherence. They try to get their like-minded judges on the bench to hear the case. Many Ahmadis are in jails waiting to be formally charged. I don't see myself ending up in a very different situation."

"Well let's hope it will be a different situation! I'll try and come back from Lahore but stay in touch in the meantime. I'll give you Jalal Ali's number where you can call me or leave a message if I'm not around."

"I will. But make sure you don't get involved. Stay out of it as much as you can. Don't ruin *your* future for a friend who has no future in this country."

We must have fallen asleep after that conversation because the next thing I remember is being woken up by a knock on the door. It was Aleem who was on round to see that everything was alright in the town. He had come to see how we were doing and to update us.

"You're still wanted, Akhtar. The *Jamiat* is after you like bloodthirsty hounds. They want you back, dead or alive. The VC has refused to file a case this morning. His office and VC house are all surrounded by *Jamiat* who are raising threat slogans. Police can be seen in television reports, but they just seem to be spectating."

Jamiat had filed a complaint with the police, and the Inspector General of the Punjab had now given a statement that they would get to the bottom of the conspiracy. He had said that the Police had already arrested some suspects who had given vital information about the conspiracy.

Aleem told me that this is how it always happened. They would always get some men to work as witnesses, and the whole case would revolve around their false statement.

"It's easier to buy a witness in Pakistan than to buy a packet of peanuts. This is how it all starts, and this is where it's going again," said Aleem.

"Why don't you hide Akhtar somewhere where he can't be found?" I asked.

"As a policy, we don't do this. We don't hide from the law. If the law decides to try us or imprison us, then we face it. Whatever the outcome."

"What law? You call this law? This is lawlessness. Sheer anarchy!"

"Whatever it is, if we stop cooperating with the law, we compromise the basis of our ideology. We can't act against the law of the land. It's against what Islam has taught us."

Aleem was firm in his approach. He fully backed his community's policy of giving in to the law if it was so required.

"Come on! They don't even take you to be a Muslim. What do you want to prove to them by acting on Islamic principles? They won't ever accept you. Never!" I was adamant.

"Religion has nothing to do with what others think. It's about what you believe. It's one's personal matter, so we make this decision to act on it in our personal capacity."

I informed Aleem about my plan to travel back to Lahore. Jalal Ali was famous for the good work he had been doing regarding Lahore's horticulture. Aleem was surprised to know that I knew him personally. He had no objections to my line of action, but he was very sure that even the likes of Jalal Ali wouldn't get involved.

CHAPTER TWENTY-EIGHT

We joined the motorway at Pindi Bhatian which would take us straight to Lahore. Aleem had arranged for a car to take me all the way to Jalal Ali's house. He had earned the wisdom of being cautious, so he had told the driver to get off the motorway at Kalashah Kaku, go through Thokar Niaz Beg and get off at Bahria Colony which wasn't far from there. This route would mean avoiding the drive through the campus.

I arrived at Jalal Ali's house quite late. It was almost ten O'clock at night. I could see the lights in the upper storey windows which meant they were about to go to sleep.

I didn't have to wait in their lobby when Shamaila came running down the stairs first. As usual, she didn't want to listen, she only knew how to hammer on and then start answering her questions herself.

Why would you just vanish when you did nothing wrong? Are you not brave enough to take a little heat? You want to bring about change; is this how people who bring change hide from the reality? And do you know how worried we've all been? But that doesn't matter to you, does it?

I had to tell her that there was nothing to worry about and that it did matter to me, a lot in fact. I had wanted to tell her all along, but the series of unfortunate events had been fast-tracked. But it was hard to make her realise that I had to talk to her father urgently.

Jalal Ali listened with reassuring attention as he very sophisticatedly took sips of his tea.

"So, how are you involved? You're just a friend, right?"

"I am just a friend, but I disappeared almost at the same time as he did. They all know we're seen together. He's accused of disappearing as soon as the alleged conspiracy was foiled. When they came round looking for me, I too had gone. They're not taking it as a mere coincidence. It's like taking the wrong causes for the wrong effect."

"I think it'll be best that you got in touch with Salim. Let *Jamiat* come to you and interrogate you.

You aren't a culprit. I have seen copies of the case that they've filed. It's only against the Quadiani students who are at large at this moment. Your disappearance for long could make you seem even more suspicious. If they drag you into this case, you'll be left as helpless as Akhtar. So try and take control of the situation. I know it's gone out of control already, but try and slip out of it while you've got the chance. You could get vital information, and that could help you and your friend."

"But, then what do I do?" I was baffled.

"Well, stay here tonight, and we can try and sort something out tomorrow. I've got the guest room ready; you can sleep there."

"I appreciate that, but sort what out? Can you not help approach the right type of people in the government? At a provincial level at the least? Akhtar is innocent. He hasn't … he just can't be part of a conspiracy!"

"Salik, let me be very frank with you. I don't think there's anything we can do to help your Quadiani friends. The Chief Minister of Punjab has issued a statement today saying that he will do whatever he can to bring the culprits to justice. Such statements only come when the pressure is immense and when the CM is left with no choice but to take some sort of action to prove his loyalty to the greater cause. Especially when it comes religious issues, they have to prove their loyalty with the proposition. Remember, we spoke about this? Now you'll get to see how it works. All I can do is give you advice on how to stay out of it. We need to know how they see you fitting in this picture. Only then can we determine how you can slip out of it."

"Sir, I don't want to slip out of it. I want to do something for Akhtar. I can't leave him alone to go through this hellhole alone. I have to stand up for him."

"Look, don't be sentimental. Stand up for your own self first. Only then can you stand up for others. I want to see you out of this mess."

I couldn't argue. Jalal Ali, the great bureaucrat, had a taller stature than mine, in every way. He was a towering personality, and I was there asking for help. He wasn't obliged to help me, but it was his sheer generosity that he did.

"Thank you, Sir. I'll come back tomorrow evening with an update."

"Won't you be staying with us tonight?"

"No Sir, I don't think there is any point staying here. I should get back to the campus, either today or tomorrow. I can't hide for something which is based on nothing but nonsense."

"I'd rather you wait for things to settle down a bit. Why can't you wait till tomorrow or another couple of days?"

"I think my absence may make things worse. I should go back tonight to see what they're up to. Thanks for your offer, but I may just avail it tomorrow."

"You know what? You're right. Go and have a look. See what's happening and keep me posted. If you need to call me, don't call me at my office. Just leave a message with Shamaila, and she'll pass it on to me."

Jalal Ali was now giving me a practical lesson of what he had just said. He stood up for himself before he could stand up for me. I didn't totally disagree with his stance. He too was an instrument of the machinery that controlled our society. He was programmed to stay where he was supposed to be.

I knew I was being sentimental by expecting him to jump into the situation and help me help Akhtar. He was good at heart and wanted to help, but only to the point where he practically could. I stopped myself from being judgmental. I wanted to continue respecting the good soul of Jalal Ali.

It was almost midnight when I left his grand villa in Bahria Colony. Shamaila was probably in bed already, so I didn't get to say goodbye to her. I walked out of the colony onto the road that led straight to the Canal Bank Road where I had to wait for about twenty minutes before the first rickshaw drove past and dropped me off at the hostel.

The route to the hostel wasn't as straightforward as it normally used to be. It had *Jamiat* guards checking who was going in and out of the campus. I had to show my university ID for them to let me in. They looked at the ID, matched the photo with my face and let the rickshaw through, which meant I wasn't 'wanted' by the *Jamiat*.

I got off just outside the hostel, crossed the road and the canal and walked towards the hostel. I wouldn't have expected too many people walking around at that time of the night, but the food stalls being almost deserted was a surprise. It meant that terror had prevailed the campus and students were not in peace. Most of them must have gone home, and those who had to stay back were in their rooms to avoid any unnecessary queries by the *Jamiat* thugs.

"Welcome back, Sir Ji!" the gatekeeper said with great fervour.

"Thank you. How have you been?"

"Good! You tell me, how have *you* been?"

There was a sly smile on his face. He knew very well that I was friends with Akhtar and he seemed inquisitive with what was going on? I didn't want to indulge in anything unnecessary with anyone, including him.

I took the stairs and went to my room. I could see that my room wasn't in the shape I had left it in. My cupboard had been searched. My clothes were all thrown out, and the drawer's lock had been picked. I opened the drawer in a rush and found that what

I had doubted was actually true. Dr Saleh's thesis was not there. *I wonder what they've done to it.* They weren't in the habit of reading, but they must have got someone to sit and read it to tell them what it was all about. My habit of highlighting certain lines and passages must have made their job easier. But those markings could make my life difficult. I had to wait until the following day to see what was going on.

I lay on my bed reflecting on what to expect. It seemed nothing like the campus I had always known. The room was estranged to me. It seemed as if I had been away for months when it was just two days. I had left the campus on 8th October and I was back tonight; 9th October. I wanted to get some sleep before I could wake up to the most eventful morning of my life.

CHAPTER TWENTY-NINE

From this point on, you know the rest of the story. It was the morning of 10th October 1999, when I was shot dead. The details of the commotion that had preceded need not be repeated. I was half awake and half asleep when I was killed.

After a lengthy discussion between the paramedics and the carefree policemen, my body was finally taken to Jinnah Hospital; the teaching hospital of the Allama Iqbal Medical College; the same college where Akhtar's brother was killed; the hospital where he had been pronounced dead, a decade and a half ago. It was the same place where Akhtar's frail father had travelled to, to collect his son's dead body.

The ambulance had to take a longer route to get there because of the many roadblocks placed by *Jamiat* on the Canal Bank Road to show their might and power.

It's strange how history repeats itself.

It was now for *my* frail father to come to Lahore, to the *same* hospital and collect *his* son's dead body. He too had hired a van and travelled to Lahore to collect a dead weight that was once his son.

It was my mother's turn to faint and collapse with the difference that unlike Akhtar's mother, she had no other son to set her expectations on. She had no reason to continue living on. She only lived for me, but I was no more.

It was my father's turn to walk with heavy steps to the police station and ask for a case to be filed against the unknown murderers. The murderers that many had seen come to my room, shoot me and walk away but no one had the courage to push themselves in the hellhole of being a witness in Pakistan's judicial system. My father was also told that he could end up in life-long interrogations if he tried to pursue the case.

He had to walk back home. He had lost all confidence in life.

Shamaila had mourned my death like no other. The lively, bubbly personality had fizzed down to a dull, grief-stricken, depressed person. We had never voiced our feelings. I knew she had deeper feelings for me than she expressed. I too had the same for her. I just wish I had told her, but we all tend to think we have plenty of time to express our feelings.

Jalal Ali had a sense of regret more than anything else. He wished he hadn't let me go back to the campus that night. He was more worried about his daughter who had lost all charm in life and had decided not to go back to a university where life was so worthless; to a place where there was no Salik.

After my murder, *Jamiat* had rallied against Dr Saleh basing their riots on the thesis that they had found in my drawer. They used it to prove that he had provided a basis to assist the Quadianis in their agenda and that I was working on its implementation. His book was released a few days after my murder and that added fuel to the fire. His office was looted, papers burnt to ashes and his house had been ransacked. So, Dr Saleh had decided to stay in the US. He had heard the news of my murder in his cousin's apartment in New York, as he got himself ready for a couple of appointments at universities.

Salim had heard the news the night before it even happened. A friend of his who had attended a meeting of the *Jamiat* had come to his room and said that the guy called Salik would not get away. *Jamiat* felt under pressure to prove the gravity of the situation and to justify the hyped up propaganda. Thus, a step had to be taken to mount more pressure on the government to punish the Quadianis severely. Salim didn't know how to contact me at that time of night. He thought he would try and contact me the following morning.

Joseph Bhatti had got to know of the news directly from the police when they arrested him from his house, as he got ready to leave for the cathedral where he worked. His house was searched, but nothing suspicious could be found. He lived in the *Delhi Darwaza* area of the walled city. He was taken to the Lower Mall Police Station for further investigation.

Akhtar had got the news in the lock-up of a Police Station where he was being charged before he could be sent to Faisalabad jail. His arrest was made at his house in Rabwah a few hours after my departure for Lahore the previous day.

He had been ruthlessly beaten with sticks, whips and canes as well as being lashed by the police who were trying to get the truth out him; the truth that they wanted to hear. He was handed a newspaper to identify my photograph that covered front page, to speak up on my connection with the alleged conspiracy. The news report read:

Quadiani Agent Killed in Punjab University Salik Hussain Qadri Assisted Quadianis in an Anti-state Conspiracy

*"(From our Correspondent, New Campus, Lahore)
It has been confirmed that the Faisalabad based
Quadiani agent, shot dead in a police encounter, played a pivotal role in the conspiracy being
planned against Pakistan. His links to Anti-
Islamic western powers have been confirmed. He
would receive foreign funds through the Lahore
Cathedral and sponsor the Quadianis who were
at work on the same conspiracy in the Punjab
University campus. He was a frequent visitor to
Rabwah, the Quadiani headquarters. He made
his last visit to Rabwah yesterday evening, where
he is said to have received instructions..."*

I was born a Muslim. I lived most of my life as an
atheist. I died an agnostic. But after my death, I was
labelled a Quadiani.

When a situation gets too complicated in Pakistan,
it's always easy to brush it under the rug of religion.

CHAPTER THIRTY

Quadianis had flocked to their mosque in the Garhi Shahu area of Lahore. It was a big building with a dome and a minaret secured with barbed wires and manned by security guards at the tall, opaque, metal gates.

They were inquisitive of the latest happenings in the nearby campus. All this seemed to be a big scale operation, and they wanted information.

An official from Rabwah had travelled to inform them and keep their spirits high. Whatever it was heading to, they had to face it bravely. The official from their headquarters addressed them after the evening *namaz*. Many of them wept in their prayers as they begged their god to come down from the heavens to help them. Akhtar had left me with second thoughts about my dibelief, but I never got the chance to sit in peace and reconsider.

As soon as the Quadiani official began to speak, the crying and wailing died away.

Everyone was shocked to learn of Akhtar's arrest and worried for his predictable future. No one knew who I was, but they were all deeply moved to hear of my murder.

But, the one person who knew me in the mosque sat in a corner, wiping his tears that rolled from his pale eyes, down his scruffy beard.

His rickshaw was parked outside the Quadiani mosque. He had given the whole day's earnings in charity. I knew he would ask his wife to pray when he got home; for my soul to rest in peace.